ICELANDER

ICELANDER

DUSTIN LONG

Grove/McSweeney's
New York/San Francisco

First published in 2006 by McSweeney's Books, San Francisco

Printed in the United States of America

FIRST PAPERBACK EDITION

ISBN-10: 0-8021-4320-2
ISBN-13: 978-0-8021-4320-4

Cover art by Josh Cochran

Grove Press
an imprint of Grove/Atlantic, Inc.
841 Broadway
New York, NY 10003

McSweeney's Books
849 Valencia St.
San Francisco, CA

Distributed by Publishers Group West

www.groveatlantic.com

07 08 09 10 11 12 10 9 8 7 6 5 4 3 2 1

For Chantal

PREFATORY NOTE

As the author of *Icelander* seems to assume at least some knowledge of Magnus Valison's *The Memoirs of Emily Bean*, I have seen fit to scatter a few explanatory footnotes wherever I felt that readers unfamiliar with that series might benefit from a bit of background elucidation. The names and biographies given in the table of Dramatis Personae that immediately follows this preface refer only to the fictionalized characters who appeared in that series and no libel is intended toward any of the real-life persons on whom they were originally based. For information regarding the disputed authorship of this novel, please see my afterword.

John Treeburg, Editor
New Uruk City, 2005

DRAMATIS PERSONAE

Emily Bean-Ymirson: That most extraordinary of women, whose diaries formed the basis of Magnus Valison's celebrated series of books. An anthropologist by profession, a criminologist by birth, she—along with her irascible but dashing husband Jon Ymirson—repeatedly demonstrated extreme proficiency in both areas until her untimely demise in 1985. Her daughter, Our Heroine, is the central figure of *Icelander*.

Blaise Duplain: Former Inspector for the Quebec City police, Duplain moved to New Crúiskeen after leaving the force. There he met Emily Bean-Ymirson and managed to lend a professional hand on a few of her cases. She returned the favor by introducing him to Shirley MacGuffin, whom he subsequently wed.

Garm: Great-grandson of the Fenris Dachshund, Garm has been a devoted companion to Our Heroine since his puppyhood.

Gerd: Queen of the Vanatru, half-sister to Prescott [see below], and rival to Our Heroine. The Refurserkir are hers to command.

Hubert Jorgen: Rogue library-scientist. Though most consider his methods somewhat unorthodox, his work remains unparalleled in the field. His radical proposal for a replacement of the Dewey Decimal System in the late 1980s led to his being blacklisted from any jobs within the mainstream library-science community, but, undaunted, he has labored on. He remains one of the world's foremost experts on ancient texts and forgeries, and at the time in which the novel is set he owned and operated the finest rare and antiquarian bookstore in upstate New Uruk.

Philip Leshio: Magnus Valison's literary agent as well as Shirley MacGuffin's. Now deceased.

Constance Lingus: A reporter who specializes in the exploits of the Bean-Ymirson clan.

Shirley MacGuffin: A continually aspiring author whose prose was matched in ambition only by its pretentiousness; best known in literary circles for her unauthorized radio adaptation of William Gaddis's *JR*. She was first encountered by the Bean-Ymirsons while under suspicion of murder, but her knack for unwittingly involving herself with less-than-savory companions kept her a close fixture in their lives until her death in January of 2001.

Our Heroine: Former professor of Scandinavian Studies at New Crúiskeen University.

Prescott: Erstwhile ward of the Bean-Ymirsons and estranged husband of Our Heroine, Prescott was born in Vanaheim and raised there until the age of thirteen. He has since returned to lead his people in their time of greatest peril.

Surt: "Surt" was the sobriquet of Emily Bean's criminal arch-nemesis. A notorious master of disguise, his true identity was never discovered, though the Bean-Ymirsons did manage to thwart his illicit activities on numerous occasions. While he was indisputably a villain in the small sense of the word, Surt was nonetheless a gentleman and lived by his own code of honor; the final volume of the *Memoirs* relates how he seemingly plunged to an icy death off the coast of Greenland rather than allow Our Heroine to be killed in an explosion that he had meant only to serve as a distraction.

Magnus Valison: One of the twentieth century's master prose stylists, Valison was born in Ghana on April 23, 1901, and descended from the original settlers of the Danish Gold Coast. He studied French and Scandinavian literature at Trinity College, Cambridge, then lived in Reykjavik and Paris, where he launched his remarkable literary career. In 1940 he moved to the United States and achieved renown as a novelist, poet, critic, and translator, though he wasn't truly to find his muse until 1980, when he made the acquaintance of Emily Bean-Ymirson. Within a year he retired to her native township of New Crúiskeen in upstate New Uruk in order to study her more closely; he died there in early 2001, following close on the conclusion of this novel's action. Among the major achievements of the first half of the Master's career are *Itallo* (1955), the surprisingly touching story of a murderous pederast, and *Ripe Leaf* (1962), in which a grand mystery blooms from the footnotes of a plant-book posthumously published by the self-styled Boswell of a respected herbologist. In the twelve years immediately following Emily Bean-Ymirson's death, Valison occupied himself almost exclusively with what is generally regarded as his magnum opus, the twelve-volume novelization of her diaries, which he matter-of-factly titled *The Memoirs of Emily Bean*.

Wible & Pacheco: Self-styled "philosophical investigators," they are best described in their own words: "We take on mundane cases such as murder and missing persons as a sideline to support our investigations into the larger Mysteries that others pass over in silence."

Jon Ymirson: Adventurer/Anthropologist. He and his family are most noted for their discovery of Vanaheim and their subsequent study of its indigenous people. Though his traditional Icelandic sensibilities often came into conflict with the vivacity of his American wife, the resultant fiery quarrels never diminished his love for her. Subsequent to Emily's death and the early onset of Alzheimer's, he has given up his career and now placidly resides in New Crúiskeen.

ICELANDER

PRELUDE

Our Heroine woke to the sound of snowflakes, plaughtting against the window, perfect stellar dendrites that shattered as they crashed against the glass. Through a too-dry throat she groaned at them—some Adamic word of banishing—but it was fruitless, and the snow's frigid spirit managed nonetheless to translate itself across the pane. From there it pressed on through blankets, quilts, and sheets to possess Our Heroine buried nude beneath. She shivered, let a yawn well through her body, and as she stretched herself out among the farthest reaches of bed, she felt the acids built up in her limbs; she felt how far she could stretch without touching anything at all.

She had not been alone upon her alcoholic fall into sleep, though she found herself so now. Hubert Jorgen was not there. The quilts and comforters curled around her still smelled of him—clean and fleshy, like soap made from bacon fat—and his head had left a pillow-dent, but the body itself was lacking. She pulled one last whiff of him in through her nostrils, and then again, across the roof of her mouth, she sounded her barbaric yawn. Song of herself.

Sliding grudgingly from the bed, then, she registered the fact that it was not her own, and she wondered vaguely how she had wound up in it. And then, through the haze of hangover, she recalled.

She'd started drinking early yesterday, hitting Hrothgar's Mead Hall as soon as it opened. Hubert had stumbled in around three o'clock.

"Have you heard?" he'd asked, tentative, perhaps unsure of how to broach such a troubling subject if she hadn't. But before she could answer he'd ordered a pint of Heidrun for himself and another for her. She'd drunk already six of the same, and the two of them continued to drink until their wallets were emptied.

Once, when Our Heroine was sixteen, she drank a couple of 250-pound Norwegian thugs under the table. Her mother had uncovered their secret smuggling ring, and they had been holding her captive in the hidden basement of an Orkney haberdashery for two days. Ever resourceful, however, she managed to convince them to play a few rounds of King's Cup—a drinking game that they had mentioned to her on the first day of her captivity—ostensibly just to pass the time.

"You'll have to untie my hands," she'd told them.

"Uh... I dunno. The boss definitely told us not to..."

"Look, are we going to play or not? I'm sure not trusting either one of you to pour shots down my gullet. Or are you scared that I'm going to overpower the two of you?"

"Ah, go on. Untie her, Haakon."

Our Heroine wrapped herself in Hubert's white robe—pulled from the hook behind the bathroom door—sheveled her golden hair into a thin black elastic that she'd left on the sink-top the previous evening, and returned to the bedroom. Standing just this side of the doorway, in a robe that was not her own, she gained new understanding of the situation. She was alone, in Hubert Jorgen's house.

All variety of villainy crept heh-hehing into her head. There were closets and drawers to rummage through, diaries to find and read, possibly some hidden stashes of pornography to peruse... The forbidden door in the basement to look behind (she wouldn't have even been curious if he hadn't expressly forbidden her to look behind it the night before; why did he always have to act so mysterious?). She had Hubert's whole physical subconscious to explore.[1] But this fancy was only fleeting, replaced almost immediately by further grim recollection. Of yesterday. Of Shirley. And suddenly

1. In the typescript, an interesting interpolation, more Valisonian than much of the text, has been stricken through: "Crawling eight years old, cramped, through passages of porous rock that crumbled beneath knees and fingers, crashing down to disrupt the final phase of Prescott's ascension—or at ten, with a twist of a rusty candelabra (cadabra, as she called it), discovering the hidden staircase in her own home in New Crúiskeen, then spiraling up to years of musty solitude and..." One wonders where this passage could have led.

Our Heroine's exploratory impulses felt frivolous, forcing her again to reappraise her situation. She was alone, in Hubert Jorgen's house.

Leaving then the bedroom and sweeping through the rest of the place did not dissolve her sense of solitude. Hubert was not in the study reorganizing his collection of Vanaheimic relics or in the library parsing the mysteries of some ancient Refurserkir tome. Neither was he in the kitchen thoughtfully preparing her breakfast. She poured herself a large glass of water. Well, then. It was time to go.

Our Heroine first met Hubert Jorgen during the case of the Reykjavik Museum Manuscript Murders.[2] Emily Bean had become convinced that someone was planning to steal *Codex No. 1005*—the *Flateyjarbók*—from the Royal Library and replace it with an exact replica, and Hubert was called in as the reigning wonder kid of the library-science world; he specialized in forgeries in general and ancient texts in particular. Fifteen at the time, Our Heroine became briefly infatuated. She'd always imagined herself marrying someone like him. Tall, thin, and bookish. Tousled brown hair and rounded glasses, leather elbows on his tweed coat, knit tie, and only ten years her elder. His attention, however, was all on Emily. At first he sneered and tried to tell her how absurd her idea was—how it would be impossible to produce an even halfway believable copy of the book, it simply couldn't be done—and even if it could, the cost involved would far outweigh any black-market

---

2. See Volume 9 of *The Memoirs of Emily Bean*.

value for the real thing. But Emily proved correct in the end, of course, and thus had begun Hubert's life-long fascination with Surt, the master forger who'd been behind the whole thing to begin with.

Her thong from off the bed and up between her buttocks—long-johns would have been wiser—then on with the rest of her clothes, as bundled as she could. She gave another glance to the flecks of snow plaughtting against the window, grabbed her fleece coat from the front hall closet, and shivered expectantly against the cold before shoving through the door.

"Wordless curses to the northern winds," she muttered; her nose felt red already. She bunched her coat up around her cheeks and pulled the door to a close behind her. As the mechanism's metal tongue slipped with a click into its cavity, she heard the phone begin to ring within. The door responsibly locked, however, there was nothing she could do.

Yesterday Our Heroine had woken to a call from Barthes down at the coroner's office. He hadn't been able to reach Duplain, he explained, and so thought that he should call her instead. And then, before she could even express her confusion, he'd told her. In all the gory detail. When she'd regained a bit of her composure, Our Heroine had thanked him—though she wasn't sure what for—and assured him that she'd do her best to find Blaise and let him know.

Blaise had finally answered his phone about four hours later.

"How has this happened?" he'd asked once he was able to

speak in articulate English sentences.

She hadn't been sure if she should go into the details with him over the phone, and so after the initial shock of the situation he'd agreed to meet with her at ten a.m. the next day—today—at the Elite Café.

The morning smelled of meat or oil behind the crispness of winter air, and the sky was a translucent gray, like fried chicken bones. Eight o'clock. Two hours to go. Across the street, the little blue building of the local store was already opening its door. She'd just have to concentrate on the shopping. For her father: stockfish, six eggs on the verge of rot, and a pint of buttermilk. For Garm, a box of meat-truffles. A bundle of peppermint for herself.

She was concentrating so intently on the shopping, in fact, that she forgot to concentrate on crossing the street; consequently, she almost allowed herself be run down by a big black car as she stepped blindly from the curb. Yet she did not allow herself to be unduly phased. "One *must* maintain composure, even in the face of utmost adversity," as her mother had always said. Picking up a small plastic handcart, she reflected that it would have done her well to recall this little *bon mot* the previous morning.

At least Barthes hadn't wanted her to come identify the body. Stabbed in the eye. Our Heroine had seen some gruesome corpses in her time, but... But this was Shirley.

She paused in the bread aisle to dry her tears.

Once, Our Heroine beat in a man's skull with a brick of gold. He'd been holding a gun on her mother in a volcanic cave in

Vanaheim. Our Heroine crept up behind him with the brick, one of many that he'd been planning to smuggle out of Iceland. She only meant to knock him out, but the first whack just made him angry, and he turned around and started choking her after the second, and he didn't let go until the sixth, and her eyes had been full of tears, and it was so dark that she could barely even see him until her mother lit the acetylene torch. And by then it was too late.

Our Heroine's father, Jon Ymirson, lived in his library. Shelves he'd hammered up from oaks he'd felled himself spanned all the walls, which were fifteen feet high and book-filled beyond saturation; Ymirson had read each word and written many himself. He'd not, however, as went the popular lore, fattened and slaughtered the very lambs that had died to vellum the parchments.

Our Heroine found him seated quietly in a chair by his unblazing fireplace, staring blankly at a pile of books on the floor, and she set her bag of groceries down beside him.

"Papa, it's me!"

"Emily?"

"No, Pa, it's me. Your daughter."

"Where is Emily?"

"She's not here, Pa."

"Where is she?"

"She'll be home soon."[3]

"I must speak to her. It is of the most utter importance."

3. Emily Bean, of course, died in 1985. It is at least odd, then, that Our Heroine would willfully deceive her own senile father on the matter.

"She and I just went shopping together. She knows how you hate shopping, so she didn't want to drag you along. I brought you some groceries."

"Oh. That is very nice of you. How much should I tip? I am not familiar with the currency here. I will just have to trust you to tell me."

"No tip necessary, Pa. I'm happy to do you such favors."

"Oh... That is very nice of you."

"I brought you some buttermilk."

"Buttermilk? But where is my wife?"

"She's in the town. Here, just a minute. I have something else for you, too. Let me get a bowl and crack these open... All right, now, take a whiff of this. What's it remind you of?"

"Hmm... It is like the volcanoes of Vanaheim. We are in Vanaheim?"[4]

"No, New Crúiskeen, Pa. Upstate New Uruk. The United States. It's Mom's home town, remember?"

"No. Some mistake has been made. I should not be here. You must fetch me my papers."

"Your papers are all in order, Pa. Don't worry. You and Mom will be back in Vanaheim soon enough. Magnus Valison—"

---

4. See also Jon Ymirson's excellent treatise on *Vanaheim and the Mechanics of a Vulcanopneumatic Society*. In a brilliant solution to the problems posed by subterranean existence, the Vanatru have for hundreds of years harnessed the heat and steam afforded by the local volcanic activity in order to provide for nearly all of their society's energy needs. Ymirson's essay is not only the standard starting point for any anthropologist or engineer interested in Vanaheim's unique system of heating and power, but it also established the guiding principles on which New Crúiskeen's own system of steam tunnels was based.

"Hmph. I have never liked that man.[5] He has always had his eye on my Emily, I am sure."

"I know, Pa. Everybody always had their eye on Mom."

"Oh, my daughter! How are you? It is so nice to see you, my dear. You appear so strange to me, though. You are looking so old and tired!"

"I'm doing fine, Pa. Thanks for asking."

"Hmm. You are welcome, dear thing. It is good news to my ears to hear that you are so fine, though. But where have you said that your mother has gone? She is not with Magnus Valison, is she?"

Magnus Valison, surprisingly enough, was fond of playing the fool. Our Heroine was thirteen when she first met him—during the L'anse aux Meadows case[6]—but he treated her as if she were three. This disappointed her somewhat, since she'd only recently read *Itallo*, and it had filled her with such readerly pleasure that she'd been compelled to plow immediately through his various other novels of the fifties and sixties—all of which she'd enjoyed—and so she'd initially been quite excited about being introduced to him. But that excitement dissolved with his first words.

"This bean appears to be sprouting quite nicely," he'd

5. Ymirson's professed animosity for the Master was one of the key factors in determining exactly which copy of Valison's will was authentic in the aftermath of this novel's events. Why would he have appointed a literary executor who hated him? See my Afterword for further information.

6. See *Would as Leif*, the seventh volume in Valison's series of novelizations of Emily Bean's diaries, and the first in which the Master himself appears as a character.

declared in his thick Danish accent.

She'd already been sensitive enough about what she perceived as her Amazonian height at that point in her life, and so this comment was perhaps not received in the same spirit in which it was intended. Still, by the end of the case, she was ready to forgive him.

Valison had been in L'anse aux Meadows doing research for a proposed novel of the supernatural. In particular, he was looking into recently reported claims of strange visitations from what seemed to be the spirits of the first Viking settlers of North America proper. New Crúiskeen being only a few hours away, the Bean-Ymirsons had been unable to resist the opportunity of debunking these reports themselves, and they had arrived in the area soon after Valison, who immediately became more fascinated with them than he had ever been with the supposed ghosts.

Emily—being a fan of Valison's work, herself—had welcomed him into their circle, and a few days after their initial meeting she and her husband had even entrusted Our Heroine to Valison's care while they went off to deal with the annoyances offered by two bungling "metaphysical detectives."

"You seem excessively fond of fidgeting," Valison had said to Our Heroine. She was sitting in an overly stuffed red velvet chair in the center of his generally garish parlor. He was sitting across from her on the red velvet couch, trying to keep an eye on her. She, of course, had been itching to help her parents with the case and so did not appreciate his dutiful vigilance.

"You are like a *brincador*," he continued, arching an implausibly tensile eyebrow.

"A what?" she asked, incredulous, readjusting herself on

the rocklike cushion.

"A *brincador*. What is inappropriately called in English a 'jumping bean.' But they do not jump. They fidget."

"Gee, thanks for the compliment," she answered.

"Ah, but it *is* a compliment. The *brincador* is a most remarkable thing, as I suspect that you are, too. Do you know how it is that it is able to fidget about, this little bean?"

"Yeah, it has a bug in it or something," she said. As she spoke, she covertly surveyed all of the room's windows with an eye for the easiest escape route.

"Well, but it is not just a bug!" Valison exclaimed, rising rapidly to his feet.

"No?"

"*Carpocapsa saltitans*," he pronounced. "It is a moth." His voice had assumed a solemn tone, and he seemed to relish wrapping his mouth around the final "o." But with a great flourish, then, he pulled a brown blanket from the back of the couch and crumpled it into a concentrated mass on the carpet in front of him.

"Um," Our Heroine said. "What are you doing?"

"The adult lays its eggs within the little bean, and—when they are hatched—the larvae hollow the core and attach themselves to it with silken strands."

Our Heroine watched, dumbfounded, while he acted out each step of this description—squatting to "lay his eggs" in the balled-up blanket on the floor, blinking dramatically as he "emerged from the egg within it," and then forming a hollow space for himself by unfolding the blanket and pulling it up by its corners to drape over his head as he stood back up again.

"Then, when some young girl innocently takes the bean

into her hand," he shouted from beneath the blanket, "the sensitive little larva within feels the poignant heat emanating from her body, and he reacts to this heat by writhing—tugging upon the threads that bind him to the bean, thus effecting the aforementioned motion of fidgeting."

Our Heroine never found out where the demonstration went from here, though, since—just as soon as Valison's eyes were covered and he began to fidget upon the floor—she took the opportunity of tiptoeing toward one of the windows and silently boosting herself through it, off to help her parents round up the criminals responsible for the false ghosts. But the performance did endear him to her a little.[7]

"Go ahead and get some rest, Pa. I just came by to see how you were doing and to bring you the groceries. I know how you always get down around this time of year, so I brought you stockfish for dinner."

"Mmm. Stockfish is my favorite."

"I know it is, Pa."

"I will cherish it always."

Despite the anticipatory rise of nausea, she continued: "There's another reason I came, too, Papa. You probably won't remember this when I leave, and it's probably best that you don't, but I should at least let you know... It's about Shirley."

"Shirley... Oh, I have always liked her."

---

7. This supposed affectionate attitude toward the man did little to deter Our Heroine's much publicized feud with Valison, in later years, over whether or not he had the moral right to novelize her mother's memoirs. Art, of course, creates its own morality.

"Yeah, she liked you, too, Pa. She looked up to you... Actually, I think she even had a bit of a crush on you, but... I'm sorry."

"It is all right, dear thing."

"No... She's— Shirley is—"

"Why are you crying, dear thing? Do not cry!"

"It's okay, Pa. Sit down. I'm sorry, I've just been trying not to think about it. I can't think about it right now. She's dead, Pa. Shirley's dead."

"Shirley?"

"I'm going to talk to Blaise today—to make sure he doesn't go off on some vengeance trip and try to find the killer himself. I thought at first that maybe I should just tell him to come and talk to you, since you know what it's like to... I mean—"

"Surt!"

"Pa... Surt's dead."

"He did this. He murdered our Miss MacGuffin."

"He's dead, Pa. I know. He died saving me."

"Hmph. I snort derisively at that, for nonetheless this is he. I warned her of him when she came to me, for he has loosed himself from Leyding before, and Dromi, as well. Fetch me my belt. I must go find him and finish this for now and ever. Though dead already he shall die again!"

"Calm down, Pa. It's okay. I don't think we should go anywhere right now. We need to—"

"I shall fetch it myself, then. For I will not have you going off to find the killer by yourself. It is not safe for you, dear thing."

"Wait a minute, shouldn't we—"

"But there is no minute to wait!"

"Okay, but shouldn't we wait for Mom? I mean, won't it be better if you're here to tell her about it? I really think she should hear it from you, so you can keep her calm. Who knows what she'll do otherwise? You need to protect her. I'll go try to find her, and I'll send her back here to talk to you. I'll let you break the news to her, okay?"

"Hmm... Yes, I see that it will be best that way. Go find her now and bring her to me."

"Okay, I'll do that. And you get some rest."

"Hmm. All right, yes. It is always nice to see you, my dear. I will let your mother know that you stopped by."

"All right, Pa. I'll see you soon. I love you."

"Yes, yes. Okay. Bye-bye, dear thing."

Outside, Our Heroine's tracks had been filled to indistinction by the snow's ceaseless fall, though fresh footprints were visible in the path she'd taken. Palimpsestuous.

She smelled smoke before she saw it, a buttery blend, brimming visibly, volubly, from Mr. Wible's short and wide pipe. Mr. Pacheco, looming thinly behind, stifled a cough as the smoke and its aroma diffused into the fog around him. Fire and water conspiring to further obscure the discernible.

"I didn't expect to see you guys here," she said.

"When flees the unknown, never are we two far behind, pursuing. Wishing not to interrupt your counsel with your father, we have been awaiting you here."

"Are you still talking like that?"

"Still we speak as always we have spoken, yes, as still you

jest too freely in the face of the Great Mystery of Death... At the moment, however, my partner and I are more concerned with another of the Major Arcana: Art. We have been given to understand that Ms. MacGuffin endowed you with certain 'documents' before her death. They are documents that I and my partner have been hired to retrieve."

"Look, I don't want to— You know, actually, I've always wondered about that. Are you guys? Partners, I mean."

"Yes, of course we are partners. But you are ignoring the thrust of our enquiry. If you possess the documents to which we refer, then we must iterate that divesting yourself of them would be to your benefit. You cannot realize their full import. They would be safer in our care, as would you if they were there."

"Wait a second. Slow down. You haven't even told me what these documents are."

"Did Ms. MacGuffin endow you with more than one set of... documents?"

"She didn't endow me with anything. But I— Ugh. Can we not do this, please? I mean, how does this case even remotely fit into the sort of thing that you guys handle?"

"The case is the world, as we have told you time over. We seek its limits, which Shirley MacGuffin has now transgressed; beyond these limits lies the metaphysical. So is our involvement warranted."

"Oh. Well, whatever; I don't have the documents you're looking for."

"Attempt not to deceive us. There is neither need for that nor hope of success. You are aware, no doubt, that certain documents were stolen from her in the weeks prior to her demise?"

"Sure, but you think I stole them?"

"No, of course not. However, we do have reason to believe that the documents with which she endowed you were related to those that were stolen, and if you were to help us—"

"Sincerely, gentlemen. I can't help you."

"The Fool. That is what you are like. Treading dangerously close to a precipice that you do not perceive. Your dog barks a warning, but you do not hear."

"Okay, that's just about the dumbest thing I've ever heard."

"Is it? Or is it the wisest thing you have ever heard?"

"No. It's the dumbest."

"Hmph. We shall see if that is true. But perhaps you will speak with less flippancy when you have realized for yourself the gravity of our statements. That we are not 'kidding,' so to speak... But for now you may go your way, separate though it may be from our own. Be mindful of what we have said, however. We have always had fondness for you and would be quite distressed if Ms. MacGuffin's fate were one that you were to share."

"Are you guys threatening me? I never took you for the Pinkerton types; I thought your spiritual path ran above that sort of thing..."

"Threatening you?"

"Well, suggesting that I might share Shirley's fate if I don't help you..."

"Oh. No, of course not. Pardon our lack of clarity. We realize only now that such a statement could be readily interpreted in more manners than one. It was our wish to mean it simply in a manner that was not a threat and which conveyed genuine concern for your safety. Though in amiability we might also suggest that it might be dangerous indeed were you to attempt this investigation on your own."

"Noted. And as long as we're being amiable, I do like the mustache, Pacheco. The grey Fu Manchu thing works for you. It does a lot for your image as a mystery metaphysician. Goes well with the trench coat."

"Your valueless flattery is not enough to distract us from our purpose."

"Duly noted. But, as pleasant as this all has been, I should really be going now."

"Of course. And in opposition to my partner, I appreciate your appreciation of my moustache. It took me quite a while to grow it out."

"Well, it was worth it. It looks good."

"The Image is the mask of Substance, but sometimes the two can become transposed."

"Okay. I'll see you guys later, then."

"Indeed you shall. Indeed you shall."

Mr. Wible and Mr. Pacheco, partners, first offered their assistance to Emily Bean during the Case of the Consternated Cossacks.[8] It all began when some southern Soviet investors decided to finance the construction of a Valhalla-themed restaurant in Vanaheim. They called in a medium to consult the local fairies before any work began, of course—they all knew the story of the famous Icelander whose whole life went

8. See Volume 5 of *The Memoirs of Emily Bean.*

to ruin just because he moved a stone from one side of the road to the other without asking for permission first. Yet although the Hidden Folk expressed mild displeasure at the prospect of relocation, they gave no warning of the deaths to come.

Problems befraught the construction from the beginning. Water finding its way into unopened bags of concrete mix, blunted ends on shovels, inexplicable breakdowns of the bulldozers... But it wasn't until the investors began to die in their homes—no discernible cause of death, yet faces frozen in mortal fright—that Emily Bean decided to apply her talents to the case. Rumors that the murders were metaphysically motivated attracted the attentions of Wible & Pacheco, drawing them thousands of miles across the globe to investigate. The local law & order pursued a more pedestrian solution, of course, focusing their suspicions on a domestic restaurateur who had been outbid by the mysteriously death-prone foreigners. It took Emily and her young daughter, however, to dig up the true killers: the fox-shirted warriors of Vanaheim.

Over her shoulder as she walked, Our Heroine noticed that a big black car had begun to follow a ways behind, moving too slowly to be going anywhere on its own. Not that she really thought anyone would be following her. It probably just had no chains on its tires. She turned up the nearest corner, regardless. She'd just take the long way to her house.

A sigh escaped her mouth as the car rolled straight through the intersection without pause. She couldn't see the driver through the tinted windows, but she supposed that was irrelevant since he wasn't following her. And who would be following her, anyways? Unless this was about Shirley, in which case the murderer might—

Never mind. The car wasn't following her, and that wasn't what she should be thinking about right now, anyway. She didn't need to solve anything; this wasn't one of her mother's mysteries. As she almost slipped in the snow, Our Heroine reminded herself that, in regard to Shirley, she was only concerned with the tragedy of someone who would never return. She was not concerned with finding some person who'd created a corpse.

But crossing then at the next corner, something big and black moved into her peripheral vision. To her left, crawling along the street immediately parallel, was the same car. Visions of Shirley's punctured eyeball popped into Our Heroine's mind, and she suddenly froze where she was; she crouched down, curling herself up in a ball of coldness in the center of the street. She did not want this.

But only for a moment. Then she raised herself to her feet—one *must* maintain composure—and walked on. Neck stiff, eyes straight, she proceeded on toward her home. Even when threatened with the extraordinary, one should never abandon the semblance of normality. Or, at least, so went one of her mother's favorite aphorisms.

By the time she arrived at her house, the big black car was nowhere to be seen.

Her front door opened without need of the key, though Our Heroine was sure that she'd set both locks. She turned and gazed at the street behind her. There was no one in sight, however, and nothing sounded amiss from within. So she stepped inside. And still nothing. Silence. No toenails tapped across the tile; Garm was gone, she realized. Or dead.

"Garm, I'm home! I have meat-truffles!"

She walked to the kitchen but found only his empty food bowl.

"Damnation!"

Water sat on the white tile. She hoped it was water, but she hadn't been there last night to let him out. The window was open. She noticed now the snow drifting in, only a few specks, but enough to account for the floor water over the course of the morning. Maybe he'd woken up and had to go and—an extraordinarily smart dog—figured out how to open the window. She shut it. No. He would have figured out how to open the door.

The door *had* been unlocked.

"Damn it. Garm!"

No response. Her home appeared otherwise in order, if a bit messy. But no indication of Garm anywhere. What could she do? Reason it calmly.

First she should make sure there were no intruders. Which would offer a more likely explanation for her open window and door. And perhaps they just had Garm with them in a closet somewhere. She closed her eyes and listened.

No noise apart from the usual sounds of the house. Quiet, but not too quiet. Not preternaturally quiet. Whoever it was must have left by now, if there had been anyone at all. And if not... She grabbed a steak knife from the kitchen and carried it up the stairs.

No one greeted her at the top, so she proceeded into her bedroom.

"Garm?" she called. She knew this was the moment at which he should have bitten the hand of whosoever held him, or at least emitted a little whimper from within his captor's hiding hole. But nothing. She threw open her closet door, just in case, but was faced solely with shoes on the floor and a jumble of hanging clothes. Downstairs, then, into the study, and up the other staircase. But all was apparently well.

Enough of this. She was alone.

So.

She'd take a bath, then. Soak and figure it all out; formulate a plan to find him.

The shower curtain was already pulled fully toward the faucet-side, just as she'd left it, thus saving her the trouble of yanking it quickly open with one hand, steak knife ready in the other. She shut the bathroom door behind herself, locked it, and then she stripped and started water into the tooth-white tub.

Her recently heavy doses of alcohol were beginning to exert some influence over her womanly form. Twisting her torso and pinching wherever possible, she perused her body in the bathroom's mirror, to make certain she was abreast of all the recent shifts in topography. Though unwelcome to her stomach and thighs, her recent gains in weight had made generous contributions to certain previously less-than-ample portions of her anatomy.

"At least two good things have come out of all this," she muttered as she stepped into the tub.

A game she used to play with Prescott: hiding in the steam, no light except the verdant phosphorescence of the ormolu lichen that subsisted on the sides of their secret subterranean *reyklaug*.[9] He always had the advantage; his nose more accustomed to excluding the smell of sulphur, he could sniff her out by the oils of her hair or the sweet excretions beading on the effusive flesh of her underarms. His own skin was nigh-albino from a life of so little sun, somehow blending with the ripple of the water—probably a trick he learned from the Refurserkir—and she could never find him by sight. Sometimes, though, on instinct alone, following some immanent clew of desire, her mouth, unsensed, would alight on his, startling lips apart with the sudden tongue she slipped between them.

She let herself go limp, now, reclined. Knife within easy reach... Her hair darkened and floating around her chin, knee-peaks angled up and out untouched by the warmth of the water that refracted the rest of her body, distorted it. Elongated torso, flattened. Her body border-straddling—real above, myth below. Just look. Black hairs that struck her as flylike marked starkly the otherwise fish-white of her shins and inner thighs. Tally marks on a page that numbered the days since she cared about shaving; she fumbled for tweezers on the shelf beside her then dug them in to remove the one or two that had tunneled pinkly beneath.

From another room the telephone rang. The dog-ransomers? A second ring. Someone in the house, with a cell-phone, trying to lure her out of the bathroom? She groaned out of the tub, grabbed the steak knife—as well as a towel from off the rack, which she wrapped around herself—and billowed out to search for the phone, which rang a third time. Not on the cradle, of course. The fourth ring came from a vaguely kitchenesque

9. The Vanaheimic word for "steampool."

direction. The dining room? No. The answering machine had it now anyway. From the living room she heard her voice.

"As you hear this, I probably either don't know where the phone is, or I'm ignoring it, so leave a message and I'll get back to you when my ignorance has ended."

"Hey, this is Hugh. I really need your help with something. I don't want to say too much on the machine, but, um... Come see me. I'm at the *home away from home*, you know? Think about Shirley. Anyway, I'll be waiting for you, so I'd appreciate it if you could get here as soon as you can. Thanks. Sorry about last night, by the way. See you soon, I hope."

Our Heroine plucked the phone from the refrigerator's top and—setting the knife down on the stove—she dialed Hubert's number.

It rang, but the bastard didn't answer. *Sorry* about last night? And how could she know where he was if he wasn't home? Stupid clues; say what you mean. At least he was okay. Just mourning in his own way, she imagined. She returned to the bathroom, pulled the plugstop from its snugness, and watched the water drain.

Perhaps Blaise would know where Hubert was. Maybe that's what the mention of Shirley meant. Our Heroine had to meet him in half an hour, anyway, so it couldn't hurt to ask. This didn't help her with Garm, of course, but at least it was *something*.

Garm's great-grandfather, the Fenris Dachshund, had insinuated himself into the life of Emily Bean during the same Icelandic vacation on which she first met Jon Ymirson. Emily was walking along the wharf, taking in the view of Reykjavik's fog-filled bay, when Ymirson stumbled backward into her and nearly knocked her into the water. Hopping one-footed, he caught hold of her with his right hand while with his left he tried to extricate his flailing leg from the jaws of the long, black Fenris Dachshund.

"Sir!" Emily had exclaimed. "For shame to enlist the help of an innocent whelp in such a crude maneuver of courtship. That is neither the way to a woman's heart nor the proper manner in which to treat a hound."

Both dachshund and man desisted and turned their eyes to Emily.

Ymirson sputtered. The Fenris Dachshund whimpered.

"Woman," Ymirson finally managed to bellow in his heavily inflected English. "This hound is not mine. He is a hound of evil who attacks my leg for no discernible reason. And the way to your heart is not—"

"Evil? You poor little thing." She squatted to gently remove the Fenris Dachshund from Ymirson's leg and then cradled him in her arms. "Perhaps, sir, if you would take more care in the future not to spill vanilla extract upon your shoes while preparing your morning cocktails, you would have greater fortune in avoiding the attentions of innocent, sweet-toothed dachshunds. Now, if you have finished harassing me and my newfound canine companion, I humbly request that you leave us in peace."

Ymirson snorted derisively, glowered, and then huffed away, leaving her and what she now called "her" dog in peace. And so went the first meeting of Jon Ymirson and Emily Bean.[10] Unbeknownst to either one of them, however, the

---

10. See the first volume of the *Memoirs* for a fuller account of these events.

Fenris Dachshund actually belonged at the time to Ymirson's chief rival, the Danish anthropologist Anders Pytlick.

The two men's mutual mentor, Clint Van Cleef—distressed by the rift between his two greatest students—had on his deathbed entrusted Ymirson with an unexplained set of geographical coordinates and provided Pytlick with a description of a landmark to dig beneath once those coordinates were reached. The two men would thus be forced into cooperation, Van Cleef had reasoned, by necessity reconciling their differences in order to locate the treasure that their mentor had bequeathed them. Van Cleef died secure in the knowledge that his pupils would thus be reunited. He had, however, never been a very shrewd judge of character.

The Fenris Dachshund was part of Pytlick's scheme to keep Van Cleef's treasure for himself. The dog had been trained to follow the scent of vanilla, which Pytlick had mixed into all of Ymirson's tins of shoeshine, and each night, the amazing canine would lead his master through every step that Ymirson had taken over the course of the day. The plan, naturally, was to wait until Ymirson visited Van Cleef's coordinates, at which point Pytlick would abscond with whatever legacy their mentor had left them. And, if Ymirson happened to arrive on the scene inopportunely or decided to cause any trouble, Pytlick always had his trusty blackjack.

The loving care that the dachshund received from Emily, however, when contrasted with the abuse he had suffered at the hands of his master, turned him firmly to her side of the struggle once she unwittingly became involved, and—in the end—he not only rescued Emily and Ymirson from a burning house but led them to Pytlick's hideout as well.

Though Garm was too young to have ever had the chance to help with any of Emily's cases—and despite a longhair or two on his mother's side—a rough eighth of his blood was that of a hero.

A staircase led up to the Elite Café from the foyer of a cinema. Steps that Our Heroine had rushed up and down twice daily one summer, still fuzzed with the same footworn carpet. She took them two at a time, now, the rail rewelcoming her hand. Nine strides, eighteen again.

The café was much as she recalled it. Brightened by skylights and wall-spanning windows, populated by the University's sundry denizens (undergrads discussing paper topics with teaching assistants, grads still rallying around their patron professors; in the least-lit corners registrars pursed their lips and drank their espressos, taking notes that no one would ever see). Our Heroine had gorged herself on this atmosphere back then. In a spiral binder she'd recorded her frustrated fantasies about the lives of these people she didn't know. How they pursued Higher Truth by day but acquiesced to Deeper Stirrings by night, playing out their academic conflicts sexually until everyone had eventually slept with everyone else... By summer's end a hundred pages had been filled with analysis of all the ideological consequences of each coupling. She generally stayed away these days and kept her literary aspirations limited to subjects she knew something about.

Blaise had chosen the place for their meeting, but he wasn't there yet, so Our Heroine stepped counterward to order herself a drink.

"Well, Professor, hello!" a voice called from behind her. It was Boris Baxter, sitting at a table with three other white men. "Have a seat."

She walked over toward his table but remained standing. "Hello, Boris. Is this all that's left of your fan club?"

"Oh, my graduate student round-table doesn't meet until one or so, if that's what you're referring to. I'll be here for the next few hours, if you're interested. But allow me to introduce Drs. Lorenz, Mohs, and Curleigh. Math, Geology, and Northern Studies, respectively. Visiting professor and two new additions to our little faculty, also respectively. I'm surprised you haven't heard. Gentlemen, this is that same illustrious doctor of whom I've just been speaking. The Bean-Ymirsons' daughter."

"A pleasure to finally meet you," said Dr. Lorenz. He was dressed rather ridiculously, Our Heroine thought—in orange pants and a green jacket—and as he spoke he toyed with a large, gaudy ring on his right hand. "Boris has told us so much, I feel as if I already know you. You're Anthropology, as well?"

"I'm something of an interdisciplinarian, actually. Linguistics, Anthropology... I'm listed with the Scandinavian Studies department."[11]

"Well, I'm something of an interdisciplinarian myself," Lorenz replied, grinning maliciously from beneath his bulbous nose. "Chaos is my specialty, but it's comprised of so many

---

11. For the record, Our Heroine's own trivial academic interests—as detailed in *The Greenland Gravestone Robberies* (Volume 12 of the *Memoirs*)—include: Iceland's enforced linguistic purity, the patronymic tradition, and the genetic purity requirement of its citizenry—the whole idea of "authenticity," as she phrases it, and just what it means to be a "real" Icelander.

things: mathematics, meteorology, lepidopterology—"[12]

"Save your mothematical monsoons," Baxter interrupted. "The trivialities of academia do not concern this one. Her criminological celebrity assures that she needn't worry about such things."

"Stop," Our Heroine mouthed.

"I suppose Ms. MacGuffin's murder was your true motivation for coming out this fine Bean Day morn."

"Stop," she said.

A pause. "Pardon me. You're absolutely right for once; I should at least honor the dead. She always was the company I welcomed most from among your bunch, and I shall sincerely miss her. A remarkable girl, Shirley. Lovely."

"I didn't know you were acquainted."

"Not incredibly well, I admit, though she and I did share a mutual affection for Saxo, and she briefly sought my help with one of the projects that she was working on in her latter days. Does that make me a suspect in your investigation?"

"So you were working with her on the—" Our Heroine began, but just then Dr. Lorenz choked on his coffee and sputtered a bit of it out across the table.

"Please pardon me, how clumsy..." he said as he quickly dropped a napkin atop the cream-clouded coffee puddle and then proceeded to pat it down with his ringless left hand.

"Why don't you have a seat, Professor?" Dr. Mohs asked. He stood and made as if to grab a chair from a neighboring table.

"No, please," she shook her head. "I'll be leaving in a moment. I'm meeting someone."

---

12. A passion shared by the Master.

"Not to indulge Boris in his rudeness," Dr. Lorenz said, looking up abruptly from his coffee-mopping, "but surely you must have some interest in the murder. I've only just read about it in this morning's paper, and I'm not nearly as experienced in this sort of thing as you... but it seems quite clearly malicious. Not just some random stab in the nearest available eye. And she was a close friend of yours, was she not? Don't you feel just the least bit obliged to lend your considerable talents to the case?"

Our Heroine faltered for a moment at mention of the eye-stab. But then she answered, recomposed.

"I haven't read this morning's article, but I'm afraid Miss Lingus[13] must have overstated my talents. I'm just a professor. And apparently not a very good one."

"But she *was* your friend," Lorenz insisted. "Surely you must care about her enough to have at least some interest in finding her murderer."

Indignant: "I cared about Shirley a great deal, I'll have you know, and I resent your suggestion that my lack of interest in finding her killer might indicate anything to the contrary. But tracking down and punishing some criminal will not bring her back to life, and bodily resurrection is about the only thing I can imagine that would make me feel better about this situation."

"Well, I do apologize for any offense I might have given," Lorenz said, rubbing the tip of his bulbous nose. "I meant only that—being her friend—you might share some connection with her in the murderer's eyes; you might be in danger

13. Despite Our Heroine's arrogant assumption, Constance Lingus did not mention her in that morning's article concerning the murder.

yourself, that is, and so solving her case might be to your own personal benefit."

"It might, but that sort of thing is what the police are for."

"Yes, of course," Lorenz conceded. "But still, you must—"

"Forgive me my tardiness," Blaise Duplain said from nowhere, behind, and laid a steady bandaged hand on Our Heroine's shoulder. "I was inextricably occupied otherwise."

"Ah. If you'll excuse me, it seems my friend has arrived. It's been nice meeting you, gentlemen. Boris."

Dr. Mohs raised his hand, slightly, and spoke before Baxter could formulate a retort. "Well, as we say in my department, rock on."

"Likewise," Dr. Curleigh said.

"Hmm. I'm afraid I must be going as well, boys," Dr. Lorenz said, rising and slapping Boris forcibly on the shoulder with his right hand as he readjusted the bridge of his nose with his left. "It's been a pleasure to meet you, though, Professor, and I do hope you'll accept my apology for any tasteless remarks I may have made. I'm sure we'll be seeing each other around. Until then, goodbye, and—as we say in my department—good luck."

"Damn it," Baxter said, scowling up at Lorenz and vigorously rubbing his shoulder where the man had slapped him. "Watch that absurd ring of yours, Lorenz. I think it might have just cut me through my jacket."

Lorenz smiled an apology as he left, and by the time Boris turned his attention back to Our Heroine, she was already sitting across the room with Blaise.

* * *

Blaise Duplain had descended upon New Crúiskeen from Quebec City in 1981.[14] He was true Quebecois, no mere Montrealer. His eyes were a frost-hued blue and his neck was darkly scruffed with a beard that he'd more neglected to shave than allowed to grow out. He had worn a black wool hat, a long leather coat to match, and brought little other luggage with him. The local tobacconist, Guy De Clerk, let him a room above the smokeshop, and perhaps Duplain conversed with his landlord, but everyone else in town he greeted only with French invective. When De Clerk was found dead, strangled with the belt of a black leather coat, Duplain found his own neck suddenly wrapped with the town's suspicion.[15] Even Emily Bean had her doubts, though eventually she did grow to trust him, and—seeing beneath his stern reticence—she assisted him not only in the capture of De Clerk's true killer but also in the resolution of his other, more personal dilemma.

Blaise sat across from Our Heroine at a table on the other side of the room from Baxter, next to a window that looked out upon the pale beyond.

"How are you holding up?" she asked him.

He lowered a bag of black tea into his clear, steam-brimming glass of water and then stared puffy-eyed at the oily red that swirled from it.

"Well, I really don't know what to say," Our Heroine said.

---

14. See Volume 8 of *The Memoirs of Emily Bean*, *Experts Texperts*.

15. Considering that Magnus Valison was killed by belt-strangulation—and only shortly after the events that this novel describes—I find such references to belts to be in exceedingly poor taste.

"..."

"You've got a little..." She reached across the table and wiped a bit of blue ink from his nose with her wet napkin. "Anyway, thanks for saving me back there. I'm like a rabbit in the headlights with him. I just can't turn away even though I know he's going to run me over."

"You are welcome," Blaise said.

She took a sip of the peppermint tea that Blaise had bought her. "You know, until yesterday, I felt as if it were all over. That after my mom died there was no way this sort of thing could happen again. I felt like she had somehow been the one who drew bad things to us. It's been sixteen years."

"Bad things have also happened in the past sixteen years. To all of us," he said.

"I know. But this is the worst thing."

"..."

"But at least you know that Shirley loved you. She didn't just leave you behind of her own free will."

Blaise gulped his tea, which was now reddened throughout.

"I'm sorry. I can't believe I said that."

"It is copasetic. Prescott was not good for leaving you behind of his own free will."

"Thanks."

"You are welcome."

"..."

"Are you—?"

"No, no. I'm sorry. I don't know why I'm like this. She was *your* wife. I just feel as if I could have— I'm sorry. I'm okay. I just can't believe any of this. I'm sorry."

"It is fine for you to cry. I value it from you."

"Okay. I think I can hold it together, now... So, you haven't heard from Hubert Jorgen, have you? I mean, since all of this happened, he hasn't gotten in touch with you, has he?"

"No, I have not heard from him in recent times. Is there something that I should have heard from him?" He ran a hand across his unshaven neck.

"No. It's just that I wanted to talk to him, and I don't know where he is. I thought you might know, because he said something about Shirley on my answering machine, and... But never mind."

"I will find him."

"No. I'm sure he's all right. It's probably nothing to worry about."

"But, if it is not nothing, then I must see him. If he has mentioned Shirley, then possibly he knows a thing about her death which will assist me in my investigation."

"See, that's the other thing I wanted to talk to you about. I know you used to be an inspector, but I think you should leave this one alone. It's too personal. Let the police take care of it."

"That is an incapability... Within the department, I think that I have something of a reputation as the hothead; it is natural that the police will suspect me of the murder—"

"That's absurd."

"In addition to its absurdity, it also has truth. And I cannot account either for where I was about when she died, and neither can anyone, for I was alone. The officers who questioned me were skeptical of this. I will be the suspect, and the trail of the true murderer will lose his musk. So I must be the one to sniff him out before. I do not wish to offend you, but

I believe that you should not attempt this investigation without me."

"Why does everyone think that I'm trying to investigate this?

"I am sorry. But regardless of whether you do or not, I am afraid that I must."

"You know, you remind me a little of my dad sometimes."

"I do not know why you say that, but it is complimentary."

"Yeah, it's good that you remind me of him, but that's why I can't— Even if I had a suspicion or an inkling about how Shirley died, I couldn't tell you about it when you're like this. Because you'd just go off and—"

"You have a suspicion?"

"I— No. But my point is... what if I had a suspect and I was wrong? My dad's the same way; if he even had a vague idea about who did this, he'd just go and—"

"I must go now. I am sorry to depart with such brusqueness, but I have wasted too much time already. Thank you for consoling me, but catching the killer will be the thing that consoles me most."

"Well, you're welcome, I guess. But you— I still wish you'd reconsider about doing this yourself."

Blaise stood, but he paused before turning toward the door. "I think I do know something of how you are miserable about Prescott. I am sincerely sorry that there is no killer to catch that would console you."

Our Heroine married Prescott in 1986. It was the summer of her first year at college and about a year and a half after her mother died. She had finally popped the question that spring—after years of tentative advances and Byronic hesitation on Prescott's part—and for once he had been decisive enough to simply say yes. It wasn't the first time that he had been a groom, however.

His half-sister Gerd had brought her Vanaheimic independence movement to the United States in 1981. After holding a demonstration in New Uruk City, she'd headed upstate to New Crúiskeen to try to recruit Prescott into the cause. She reasoned that he—as the hereditary leader of Vanatru society—would be able to gain greater international recognition for Vanaheim's plight than she alone had managed thus far. At first she just tried to explain the politics of colonialism to him in the simplest terms possible, but when that failed to arouse his passions, she'd decided to play more on the issue of his heritage, trying to convince him of how much he'd been deprived of by being raised in America. In his homeland he was a god; here, he was a sidekick. This approach proved far more successful.

Prescott was eighteen years old at the time, and he'd already been developing an interest in exploring his roots. Our Heroine tried to convince him that Gerd must have some ulterior motives in mind, and that he shouldn't trust her, and that he was being played for a fool. But this had only angered him and quickened his resolve. Within a few days, then, he had agreed to fulfill his arranged and long-delayed marriage with Gerd, as a show of respect for the customs of his people. Gerd did indeed have her own vested interest in the matter; the marriage promised to reinforce not only the legitimacy of her cause but also her own legitimacy as Vanaheim's self-appointed monarch, which only added, of course, to the fact that she claimed to love him.

This had been around the same time as the murder of Guy De Clerk, and while Our Heroine had busied herself with trying to convince Prescott of Gerd's malevolence, Emily had been attempting to prove Blaise Duplain's innocence. At first, they each refused to help the other, which caused some degree of annoyance for both parties. Yet once all the facts had come to light, mother and daughter discovered that they'd actually been working on the same case the entire time, and with the help of Skoll—son of the Fenris Dachshund—they managed to overcome their differences, break up the wedding, and catch De Clerk's true killer before he could get away.

Prescott had never completely given up his devotion to the cause of Vanaheimic independence, of course—no matter how little he understood of the details of the situation—and when for reasons entirely mundane he and Our Heroine had separated in July of 2000, he'd moved immediately back to his native land to embrace the deification that Western Society had long denied him. And it wasn't long after this that he'd embraced Gerd, as well.

Our Heroine remained at the table and gazed out the window, down through her pale, pellucid reflection. She saw a small dog skulking near a steaming sewer grate. A fox, rather. Not Garm. Blaise emerged from the door of the cinema below. Our Heroine turned her eyes up, from him, and watched wisps of gray smoke rise in the distance, watched the snow *continue* down, as if it were all the same snow and still involved in the same fall instead of discrete flakes involved in falls of their own... Indecipherable hieroglyphs sent from the sky. She'd always been good at seeing the hidden meaning in things, but no matter how closely she looked, she couldn't make any sense of these.

Once, Emily Bean told Our Heroine that she loved her. She'd been driving—Our Heroine in the passenger seat—toward a New Uruk City bank that, as they'd recently discovered, was holding Arne Saknussemm's[16] encrypted notes in an anonymous customer's safety deposit box, and which they suspected Surt might therefore attempt to rob. Forgetting the clutch, Emily—who had only taught herself to drive earlier that year—had just forced the T-bird's gearshift into first and then managed to shake it to an engine-dying halt along the curbside, narrowly avoiding collision with an old woman in mourning and her husky Boy Scout companion, both of whom were standing beneath a sign that read PEDESTRIAN XING and waiting to cross to the street's other side.

Our Heroine's first thought as she lifted her five-year-old forehead from the face of the glove compartment was of amazement that the concept "to cross" could be conveyed by having the two lines of the letter "X" intersect with each other—it was her first English ideogram—and she told her mother how clever she thought it.

"But mother," she continued, "I just don't see what's so pedestrian about this crossing. Considering the fact that it doesn't coincide with any intersection of roads, not to mention

16. Sixteenth-century Icelander who is purported to have discovered an underground realm that may or may not have been connected to Vanaheim. See Volume 2 of the *Memoirs*, *The Case of the Backwards Bookshelf*, for the full details of the events referred to here.

those men in silly costumes within it or the pleasant shade of this displaced eucalyptus looming alongside it, I would say that this crossing is quite droll."

This was when Emily had said the three words and leant over the gearshift to kiss her, smearing crimson lipids across Our Heroine's snow-cold cheek. Emily had had to explain the *other* meaning of the word to Our Heroine much later, because immediately after this she realized that the old woman and the Boy Scout now entering the bank were actually Surt and his dwarfish cohort Draupnir in disguise.

"Let's go," she said, grabbing her daughter by the wrist and pulling her out the driver's side door.

Our Heroine left the Elite Café, reluctant only to lose its warmth, and headed down to the bustling Telegraph Avenue of Bean Day. She was uncertain of where she should go next, though she knew that she didn't want to linger in a place where Boris would be in residence for at least the next few hours. She decided just to start walking, and she would think about her destination as she went.

At the corner of Telegraph and Dixon, then, she stepped down from the curb and into the Xing, musing as she did so that she probably ought to stop by Hubert's store—which was just around the corner, really—and see if he was there. To make sure he was okay. But then before she could make a final decision she was once again almost run down by a big black car.

Luckily, she was tackled into a snowbank before the car could hit her.

"Are you okay?" asked the young man sitting in the snow

beside her. "That guy just came out of nowhere."

She glanced first to him and then to the car, which was already veering around the next corner. And then she looked up at all the pedestrians looking down at her.

"Yeah, I'm fine," she answered. "Thanks."

"Hey, wait a second; are you who I think you are? I mean, you're not just an impersonator, are you?"

"If you think I look like someone worth impersonating," she said, rising and brushing the snow from her clothes, "then I'm probably who you think I am."

"Wow," he replied as she grabbed his hand and helped him to his feet. "It's really cool to meet you. You can call me Nathan, by the way."

The tourists were already starting to pull out their cameras.

"Nice to meet you, Nathan," she said. "Nice of you to tackle me, actually. But maybe we could discuss this as we walk."

"What?" he asked. And then he seemed to register all the interested onlookers. "Oh, yeah. Sure."

She watched more carefully this time as she left the sidewalk and then headed up Dixon, Nathan trotting behind.

"I suppose you must get that all the time," he said.

"What, attempted hit and run? Well, more than I'd like, but I'm hoping that particular lunatic at least won't try to run me down again with you along as a witness to his latest attempt."

"I just meant the cameras."

"Oh, that. No, not really. Only on Bean Day, actually."

"Well, you should consider yourself lucky. It seems like my fans never take a holiday."

"You have fans?" she asked.

He stopped walking before he answered, and she stopped with him.

"All right... are you kidding?" he asked. "I'm not trying to sound cocky; I really just don't know if you're kidding or not. Do you really not know who I am?"

She looked him over. Blue eyes, brown hair and the scraggly beginnings of a beard. Not bad looking... but completely unfamiliar. He was no one who had ever tried to kill her, at least.

"I can honestly say that I have no idea who you are."

"Wow. This is great. This is perfect."

"Should I know who you are?" She started walking again, and he followed.

"No. No. Absolutely not." He sliced his hand through the air as if to knock the notion from the table of imagination. "I'm just upstate for Bean Day, you know, to celebrate the anniversary of your mom's death—or to honor her life, I mean—but I think it's wonderful that you don't know who I am."

"So you're a fan of the books, then?"

"Well, yeah. And I'm a big fan of you in particular. I mean, I know I don't know you, and you're not the you-from-the-books, but... Well, you're my favorite part of the books. You're a big part of why I accepted this gig on such short notice, in fact."

"Gig?"

"Yeah, me and a few other authors are speaking at the Valison panel later on. You should come watch. It's a pretty big deal, I guess, because Valison himself is supposed to be there, and, you know, it'll be his first public appearance in like three years."

"Yeah, he doesn't get out much anymore. Especially in winter. Icy ground is the natural adversary of the walking stick."

"Wow, yeah, I forgot you actually know him. How old is he, anyway? Like a hundred something?"

"He's getting up there. He's always been pretty spry for his age, but I think it's finally started to catch up with him over these last few years. But so you're a writer, then? Maybe if you told me what you've written—"

"Trust me, you wouldn't know me from my fiction. In fact, modesty compels me to tell you that—while, yes, I am technically a published novelist—it would be misleading to describe myself as a *real writer*, you know. Nothing to compare with Valison, at least. But, yeah, it would be closer to the truth to say I'm just an actor who happens to write. Which I think is the real reason I was invited here today... I mean, I'm sure my literary agent didn't hurt, either, but... Well, hey, whatever the reason, I couldn't turn down free Bean Day accommodations, could I?"

"I suppose not," Our Heroine replied.

Bean Day had first been celebrated only after Magnus Valison's *The Case of the Backwards Bookshelf* had become an international bestseller. Before that, no one had shown much interest at all in honoring the life of Emily Bean. Our Heroine tried not to be too angry with Magnus himself about all of this. It wasn't his fault that his fans were a little rabid, and she trusted that he had written the books with only the best intentions in mind. But every Bean Day made it a little harder to hold her anger in.

The candlelit vigil at the grave was appropriate enough, she supposed, but Our Heroine found everything else to be just a bit demeaning. Fans dressing up alternately like her best friends and her worst enemies, taking over the town as they wandered through all the sites of her family's various local misadventures... Our Heroine always felt that they were treating her mother more like a favorite fictitious character than the real and amazing woman she was.

Some enterprising townsfolk had even set up exhibitions and rides. These ranged from the merely annoying—such as the tour buses, which put the private homes of Magnus Valison, Our Heroine, and her father on public display—to the tasteless—such as the "Vanaheim Tunnel of Love" indoor boat-ride, the "Viking Relic Scavenger Hunt" in Bean Memorial Park, and the theatrical adaptations of Valison novels put on by the local drama troupe, wherein audiences were treated to caricatures of Our Heroine in all of her various stages of awkward youth. Worst of all, though, had been in 1995, when some overzealous fan had paraded a giant balloon version of Our Heroine down Main Street; she had always tried her best to spend her Bean Days indoors after that.

Our Heroine's mouth still back-tasted of alcohol, so she sucked a mint leaf. But the first flavor lingered. Sour, and the diffuse smell of chimney smoke in the air all around only reminded her of how cold it was. Nathan coughed emphatically into his hand as he tried to keep pace with her.

"So where are you off to?" he asked. "My agent mentioned that there was a murder in town yesterday. Are you investigating?

I mean, was that car trying to hit you intentionally, to stop you from finding the murderer or something?"

She slid the leaf beneath her tongue, thought, and then swallowed it. "You have a vivid imagination. But no. I'm just looking for my dog."

"The Fenris Dachshund, right? I love the Fenris Dachshund."

"This is his great-grandson, Garm. I love him, too."

"But there really was a Fenris Dachshund. That's wonderful. I've never known what to believe and what not to believe about your mother's memoirs.[17] Everything in them seems so fantastic, I'm never sure how much is Magnus Valison's embellishment and how much is just fantastic shit that actually happened to you guys."

"I'd really rather not talk about the *Memoirs*."

"Oh yeah, you and Valison don't get along, do you?"

---

17. Such loose usage of the term "memoirs" has been a common point of confusion among many readers of Valison's novels. Some have even labored under the misapprehension that Emily Bean was an entirely fictitious character and that the diaries upon which Valison based his most famous series were merely created by him as a dramatic device. This is a perfectly understandable assumption, as many of the Master's earlier novels employed such techniques as fictitious editors and imaginary source material. The fact remains, however, that Emily Bean was indeed a real woman, that she recorded all of her adventures in a multivolume field diary, and that Magnus Valison used that diary as the basis for a series of twelve novels that he published in the years following her death and which he titled *The Memoirs of Emily Bean*. Now, as to the simpler question of how *closely* his novels adhere to their source material, one can only speculate. The Master undoubtedly added a great degree of dramatic tension and linguistic artistry that would have otherwise been lacking, yet he also always insisted that everything in the *Memoirs* was true. Of course, he also claimed that Art was its own Truth, so this previous statement may not be as straightforward as it seems. Yet in basic outline, at the least, the *Memoirs* are based in fact.

"On the contrary, we get along quite well. He's kind of like an uncle to me. We did have a minor disagreement about whether or not he should make novels out of my mother's diaries, but[18]— In any case, I haven't read the *Memoirs*, myself, so I'm afraid I can't help you."

"Okay, but you know what was real, even if you don't know what was written. The two of us collectively could probably piece together everything... I mean, for instance, the arch-villain of the *Memoirs* is this guy called Surt. So how does that compare with reality? Was there a Surt? A real, individual person, like an actual master of disguise, criminal genius, etc., etc.?"

"Yes."

"You're not just messing with me, are you? Because I kind of had this theory going that he was supposed to be a symbol for the evil that men do. Like all the different disguises that he takes show how evil can take many forms, but that, despite all the different personas, the same face of primal, archetypal evil always lurks just beneath the surface."

"Nope. He was real."

"Wow."

Steam rose from a grate down to the tunnels and smelled of rotten eggs.

"But my father pretty much thinks of him as the living embodiment of all evil, even though he's dead. If that's any comfort."

"You know, I met your dad once, but I didn't even realize it was him until too late."

18. A pointless argument, it seems to me, since as the Master pointed out in an early essay on the Kalevala, "Art is justified by its own morality."

"Yeah? When was that? He doesn't get out much these days. He's not as old as Valison, but..."

"Well, it was about three years ago, I guess. When I was visiting Vanaheim. I met Gerd, too, while I was there. She was a lot nicer than Valison made her out to be in the *Memoirs*. So I guess it wasn't all true. She was giving this speech about Vanaheim's attempt to gain independence from Iceland and stuff. We talked a little afterwards because she thought maybe my status as a big-name actor could help the cause. You know, like I could do a benefit or something to raise awareness."[19]

Our Heroine quickened her pace.

Our Heroine's adversarial relationship with Gerd began almost immediately upon their first meeting in 1976, during the case in which the Bean-Ymirsons discovered Vanaheim.[20] The family was living in a small Icelandic village near Snaefells and had become intrigued by the profusion of local legends concerning beings that the villagers referred to as "the

---

19. Magnus Valison's exact feelings on the issue of Vanaheim's sovereignty are difficult to discern. Though Gerd was a featured antagonist in a full fourth of the twelve volumes of the *Memoirs* (implying at least some sympathy on Valison's part with her Icelandic detractors), Valison's views as expressed in his nonfiction works are unabashedly pro-Vanaheim, often evincing the opinion that topside Iceland—having endured the colonial yoke of Denmark for an even longer term than his own native Ghana—could not be forgiven for assuming the oppressor's role itself. In some instances, he even seems to advocate violent overthrow. As he writes in *A Sodomite Cookbook*, "We await the day that Vanaheim, like an unruly footnote, will rise to overwhelm the would-be master text of topside Iceland."
20. See Volume 3 of the *Memoirs*.

hidden folk." Ymirson initially took this all to be nothing more than indication of a rich folkloric tradition, but when Our Heroine had gone off exploring on her own one day and fallen through a hidden opening in the ground, the Bean-Ymirsons were soon made aware that some of the legends were only too true.

Our Heroine knocked herself unconscious in the fall, but fortunately Prescott had been wandering Vanaheim's outer regions at the time—sulking over the constraints of the life that was laid out for him after his impending ascension to the throne—and he heard her come crashing down. He'd never seen a topsider before, so he smuggled her into his living quarters without a word to anyone else lest they take her away from him.

The Bean-Ymirsons searched for her frantically over the next few days as Prescott nursed her back to health; they'd almost given up hope by the time the locals began to suggest that perhaps she's been kidnapped by the hidden folk. Despite their natural skepticism, Jon and Emily were by that point willing to try just about anything. Through continual bellowing, then, Ymirson was finally able to convince the locals to take him to Vanaheim.

From there, things got really complicated, with the rumblings of a not-so-dormant volcano, an ill-fated love affair between a local girl and a wayward Vanatru youth, and Ymirson's chief assistant Jonsi hatching an elaborate plot to murder the family and lay claim to the discovery of Vanaheim for himself. To this end, he managed to enlist the cooperation of Prescott's uncle Bragi, who had long planned on ruling Vanaheim from behind the scenes after Prescott's ascension, anyway.

Gerd got involved in the plot, as well, once she found out that Prescott was keeping Our Heroine in his quarters. Personal motives aside, she firmly believed in upholding Vanatru tradition; she thus considered all topsiders to be the enemy, and so felt she had no choice but to go along with Bragi and Jonsi's plan.

The Bean-Ymirsons eventually brought everything to a happy conclusion, of course. Bragi fell to his death in an attempt to stop Our Heroine from disrupting Prescott's ascension, Jon Ymirson foiled Jonsi's scheme and turned him over to the authorities, Emily Bean convinced Gerd of the error of her ways, and the family adopted Prescott, bringing him back home with them to the States rather than leave him to the mercies of his uncle's remaining supporters. True, Gerd had popped up on a few occasions since then to cause trouble for Our Heroine, but for the most part things had worked out well for everyone involved. At least up until the last six months.

Vico Road, on which Hubert's shop was situated, was at least well plowed, though the snow still annoyed. Flakes drifting back and down and forth, to hit the ground, like space invaders in the cinema lobby that summer.

"It must be so cool to have a whole town celebrate your mom every year," Nathan offered as they walked past a street-vendor's table laid with complete sets of the *Memoirs*.

"Which Bean Day attractions have you visited so far?" she asked.

"Well, not many, to tell the truth. I kind of got a late

start on this whole thing, since my literary agent didn't even call me to tell me about this gig until yesterday, and I had to drive up late last night. I've only been with him for a little while now, since my old agent died of food poisoning, and so we still haven't quite worked out the kinks of communication, you know. Let's see, I did have a cup of ormolu tea when I woke up this morning, though. And I bought a ticket to the "Discover Vanaheim" exhibit at the museum this afternoon."

"Didn't you say you've already been to the actual Vanaheim?"

"Yeah, but this exhibit's supposed to compress the whole experience into about half an hour, so I figure it'll be pretty intense."

"I'm sure. Anyway, here we are."

Dust-encrusted curtains cut the interior from view through the window, but darkness beamed beneath their edges. He was probably in there hiding.

"And where is here, exactly?" Nathan asked.

"This is a book-store. It belongs to a friend of mine. Hubert Jorgen."

"And you think your dog might be in there?"

"Just as likely here as anywhere else, I suppose. It's *kind of* a home away from home."

"All right. Should we break the window, then?"

Our Heroine glanced up at him. He seemed serious.

"Let's try the door, first," she suggested.

"Ah. Right."

The door swung open with a bell-tinkle to further expose the lack of light within. Our Heroine glanced around. The street seemed pretty empty. And no one peering down from any windows. But then she saw: Wible's pipe spilling smoke around the corner down the block. Well, so what if *they* were following her. She turned back to the door.

"Hubert?" she called. "It's me. And I've brought a friend."

"Doesn't look like anybody's in there," Nathan said.

"Hubert, are you here?" Her words went echoless, absorbed by the books.

"Shut the door," she said to Nathan as she stepped into the store in front of him. "The light switches are in the back; I'll go get them."

Hands out front, sliding her feet along the floor so she wouldn't trip, Our Heroine faded into the ash-colored quarter-light of the store's far end. When a shelf got in her way she cursed, glanced back at Nathan's silhouette against the yet-open white rectangle of doorway, then turned and moved on. Nothing sounded, aside from her shuffling. Finally she found it, cold concrete wall and rusty metal box on it; careful not to cut herself she reached inside and flipped the switches.

"Can I come in now?" Nathan called beneath the new fluorescence.

"Yes. And I told you to shut the door." This time he did.

She found the key to the back room in a drawer beneath the cash register, attached to a plastic keychain bauble shaped like an Arctic fox. Hubert's silly little fascination.

"Stay here a minute. Browse," she said.

"Will do," he replied, kicking the unswept floor and gazing up at the books above.

A smell hung in the back room like the mildewed towel beside the sink. Not good for antique books, though most of the piles on the floor just looked like modern firsts.

"Hubert? Are you even back here?"

She climbed the ladder to his workspace. Not there, either, but the desk lamp was on. A relatively new looking hardcover book and a few loose, older pages lay between his restoration tools and an ancient black rotary phone. She pulled a mint leaf from the plastic bag in her fleece pocket and curled it beneath a molar.

The loose pages looked like vellum, though she was far from an expert. Writing scarcely visible through the brown of age, she was afraid to touch the sheets lest they crumble. What she could make out, however, looked Vanaheimic. Possibly Old Norse, but—

The ladder creaked behind her.

"Hey, this is a cool little room," Nathan said, poking his prairie dog head through the ladder hole.

"I thought I told you to stay down there and browse."

"Yeah, I was browsing, but then it occurred to me that I probably shouldn't touch anything... You know, the books being rare and therefore probably fragile. So I figured I'd be better off up here under your supervision. What's that you've found?"

"Nothing related to Garm. Looks like pages from some old book Hubert was restoring. Or maybe something he was checking to see if it was a forgery, since that was sort of his specialty." Squinting: "As near as I can tell, it's a history of Denmark... Shit."

"The *Historia Danica*?"

She turned her head to him in surprise but then looked back to the pages. "No. Not exactly. At least not the one

I think you're thinking of..." As she spoke, though, she happened to glance at the book beside the pages.

"But that's odd," she said.

"What's odd?"

"Well, these pages aren't from the *Historia Danica*—they're not even in Latin—but this looks like a modern copy of the *Historia Danica* right here beside them..." Then, looking up at him: "How do you know about this stuff, anyway? I mean, you don't exactly strike me as the most likely Saxo buff."

"Well, I played Hamlet a couple years ago."

Our Heroine felt a slight shiver in her neck, and she turned her eyes back toward him. He still looked harmless enough. It was probably just a coincidence. Besides which, she wasn't investigating anything, so what did it matter to her if it wasn't a coincidence? But still, considering what Shirley had been working on before she died...

"So playing Shakespeare's Hamlet inspired you to read the Saxo version of the story in the *Historia Danica?*" she asked him.

"Yeah," he answered. "I mean, a translation of it, anyway. Just to get into the role, you know, that being the earliest extant version of the story and all. But really, the only reason I've even heard of Saxo or any of that stuff is because I read about it in *The Memoirs of Emily Bean*. Surt's schemes always revolved around some obscure piece of Scandinavian trivia like that. Or the pseudonyms he used would have some esoteric meaning that was supposed to clue your mom in that it was him. But I guess you know that, don't you?"

* * *

The arch-criminal known as Surt first crossed swords[21] with the Bean-Ymirsons on the case of the Backwards Bookshelf and continued to plague them until his fatal plunge into the Arctic Ocean during the case of the Greenland Gravestone Robberies. His crimes ranged from the bootlegging of beer in Reykjavik during prohibition to the murder of a former Danish viceroy. But the crime that pleased him most was undoubtedly the addition of his sobriquet to the *Icelandic Book of Settlements*. Despite her philosophical opposition to him, Emily couldn't help admiring his genius.[22] Jon Ymirson, on the other hand, restrained himself from such admiration quite easily.

Our Heroine followed Nathan out of the shop and then slammed the door shut behind herself.

"Where to, now?" Nathan asked. "I mean, I still don't get why we're checking shops if we're looking for your dog, but— Hey, isn't that the car that almost hit you?"

She turned to see that he was correct. Her first instinct was to run away. But then she realized how absurd that instinct was. The car was parked. She could at least write down the

21. An apt choice of cliché, for once, compared to all of the "derisive snorts" and "malicious grins" found elsewhere in the text. The mythological character from whom Surt derived his *nomme de crime* is neither one of the Aesir (the central deities of mainstream Norse theology) nor one of the Vanir (the central deities of Vanatru theology). Rather, he is a singular primal being from the fiery land of Muspellheim (somewhere south of the inhabited world), where he silently awaits the advent of Ragnarok, the day on which he will reforge his flaming sword and with it fell the dead hollow form of Yggdrasil that new life might grow in its place.

22 A common topic of debate among Valison scholars is whether or not genius was the only aspect of Surt that Emily Bean admired.

license plate number. And why not confront the driver, if he happened to be there? What could he do, shoot her? Still, it took a moment for her feet to move.

A man got out of the car as she and Nathan approached.

"What ho!" he called.

"Hey, that's my agent," Nathan said.

It was Philip Leshio, literary agent both to Magnus Valison and Shirley MacGuffin. And apparently Nathan, as well.

"Fuck," Our Heroine said aloud, perhaps a bit annoyed at having her sense of imminent peril resolve into this particular banality.

"Good to see you arrived all of a piece, Nathan, old boy," Leshio drawled Oxonian. Our Heroine knew that he lived and worked in New Uruk City. She'd never established whether or not he actually had any connection to Oxford.

"Hey, Phil, I was going to call—"

"Why have you been following me?" Our Heroine asked before Nathan could finish his sentence.

"Hello? What's this? Following you? Do try to make sense, old thing." He was shivering against the innards of his thin gray suit, too slim himself to fend the cold from his bones. "I'm simply thrilled to see you, of course, but—"

"You almost hit me with your car. Twice."

"By Jove, was that you? Both times? Yes, well, I certainly understand how you might have misinterpreted my intentions, and I offer my apologies on that score, but pedestrians do tend to look rather similar when one is attempting to gain control of a hydroplaning motor vehicle. I neglected to fit my tires with chains, you see. But dash all that for now; I have a most urgent matter to discuss with you. It's to do with Shirley, and that *Hamlet* project of hers."

"Hey, we were just talking about—" Nathan began.

"Wait a minute. That's not a satisfactory answer," Our Heroine interrupted. "Even if you didn't mean to almost hit me—twice—I've still seen your car almost everywhere I've gone today. And I want to know why."

"Indeed! Well, yes, indeed it must seem rather more than a coincidence... But we'll just save discussion of it for tonight, shall we?"

"Tonight?"

"Hrothgar's Mead Hall. Did Angus not get in touch with you? No? Tut-tut. Well, a few of us were contemplating a little whatsit there, tonight, circa eight o'clock. Angus will be on hand, similarly 'Mutt' Sanders, as well as an old professorial chum of mine by the name of Lorenz. Likely a few others, too. Nothing formal, just fishing in the void for meaning in all of this, with Shirley, of course, as the vertex of our anglings."

"Who's Shirley?" Nathan asked.

"I met Lorenz today," Our Heroine said. "But who's this 'Mutt' Sanders?"

Leshio grinned maliciously. "What say I just introduce you to him tonight. I can count on you being there?"

"Well, if Angus is going to be there—"

"Smashing. I must be popping off, now, but I'll see you later," he started back toward his car. "Oh, and Nathan... Hadn't you better be popping off, as well?" He tapped his watch as he climbed into the driver's seat. "The panel begins in half an hour." With that, he closed the car door and pulled away from the curb.

"Oh, shit, he's right," Nathan said, pulling a cell phone from the pocket of his jeans and glancing at the face. "I totally lost track of time."

"I guess you'd better be going, then," Our Heroine said.

"Yeah, but look, it was really nice to meet you. And I'm really sorry my agent almost hit you with his car. Good luck finding your dog, though, and maybe I'll see you later, okay?"

"Maybe," she replied. But she wasn't thinking about Nathan or Garm or even Hubert at that point. She was more concerned about Angus.

Our Heroine first met Angus O'Malvins during one of her mother's final cases:[23] the search for Magnus Valison. He had disappeared in a rather unspectacular fashion. At first everyone just assumed that he'd gone off to research some new novel or visit friends abroad, and that he'd simply forgotten to tell anybody where he was going. But then a few weeks went by, and nary a postcard was received. So—rather than alert the police—Emily decided to investigate.

Our Heroine helped her search Valison's house. She was sixteen at the time, but skinny enough—despite her height—that squirming through cat-doors posed her little problem. Once within, however, the two of them encountered another obstacle: the complete lack of anything mysterious.

To all appearances, Valison had gone on vacation. Tacked to his message board was a note in his handwriting that read, "Call Emily about watering my plants!" On his desk,

23. With some minor differences of detail, the "case" that follows apparently corresponds to Volume 10 of the *Memoirs*, *Et in Orcadia Ego*.

they found a confirmation number for a flight to London, and next to it the address of a local pet hotel for his Siamese. He had taken his bags with him, as well. Everything appeared to be in order. Perhaps too orderly, in fact, and Emily wasn't convinced.

So she and Our Heroine rummaged through the entire house, from his bathroom cabinets to the garbage bins in his basement. Yet still the only even semi-interesting scrap they came across was a torn-up envelope that had been mailed about a month earlier from an address in Kirkwall, capital city of the Orcadian Archipelago. Of course, neither Our Heroine nor her mother could think of anything significant or sinister about the Orkneys (at least with regard to Valison), but—arrogantly faithful in the power of her own intuition—Emily thought this scrap enough to go on, and she bought plane tickets for the entire family plus Prescott to leave that night.

She had to tell Ymirson that a group of primitive Norsemen had been discovered living in isolation on one of the remoter islands in order to get him to go, and he tried to turn the plane around himself when he found out the truth. But by the time they reached Kirkwall, he had resigned himself to helping her.

The address from the envelope led them to a small house near St. Magnus's Cathedral, and it was there that they found Angus.

"Why, hullo thair, and whae are ye?"

After brief introductions, he explained that, yes, he and Valison had known each other in their days at Trinity, where, in fact, they'd become fast friends after independently ascertaining that they were anagrammatical twins. But Angus had left Cambridge after graduation to become a customs clerk up here in the islands, and he hadn't seen Valison since their days in university; he'd come to Kirkwall, after all, primarily to indulge his hermitic bent and focus on his poetry.

"Well, what was it, then, that prompted you to contact him last month and summon him here?" Emily wanted to know.

But the fact that Valison might be in town was as much a surprise to Angus as was the scrap of envelope bearing his own address that Emily promptly produced, especially considering the fact that Angus had never once written Valison a letter. Emily took this as a promising sign; it deepened her conviction that there really was a mystery in need of solving. Jon Ymirson only snorted.

Of course, Angus said, he'd be glad to offer up any help that he could, and Emily considered this sufficient invitation to transform his little house into her base of operations. Our Heroine got to sleep on the living room floor.

Several days passed without a lead. Eventually, though, Emily managed to stumble across a needlessly baroque smuggling scheme being run out of a small haberdashery in Stromness, the other big town of the island. Someone was trying to replace the local megaliths with concrete replicas and move the originals up to Norway. He might have succeeded, too, if his henchmen hadn't been quite so inept. At least he was wily enough to not get captured, himself.

Between keeping an eye on accident-prone Prescott and escaping from drunken Norwegians, Our Heroine grew rather fond of Angus. The entire family did (excluding Jon Ymirson, of course, who believed that Angus had designs on Emily). Prescott was just impressed by the man's ability to pull coins out of people's ears, but Our Heroine even opened up enough to let him read some samples of her own early forays into the realm of fiction. It was with considerable trepidation, then, that she first began to suspect him of involvement in the smuggling ring.

Eventually, to her great relief, the mastermind behind the plot wound up being one of Surt's former lieutenants of crime, who also happened to have been a lower-classman from Valison and Angus's upper-classman days. He'd apparently held something of a grudge over the years for all of the sophomoric abuse that he'd suffered at their hands, and his extended plan had been to frame the two of them for stealing the megaliths, thus achieving his revenge while at the same time providing the police with a scapegoat for his crime. It had been he who'd summoned Valison to the Orkneys, and he'd also abducted him soon after his arrival. Emily's intuition had once again wound up proving true.

Angus had been called away to Glasgow to pray at the side of his dying mother before the family even figured out where Valison was being held, but not before he had been cleared of suspicion in Our Heroine's eyes. Their parting was a tearful one on both sides, and the two of them had never quite lost touch with each other. In later years, she'd even introduced him to Shirley MacGuffin, who came to regard the man as something of a mentor, though she rarely had the temerity to let him read any of her writing. But he'd liked her too much to offer useful criticism, anyway.

Our Heroine followed Vico Road west, farther from Main Street and the stations of Bean Day and back in the direction of her home. She needed a place to sit and think things through logically. It was impressive, she mused, that Angus had managed to hear about Shirley's death and make it all the way to New Crúiskeen from the Orkneys in less than two days. And he *had* helped Shirley somehow with her *Hamlet* project while she was in Denmark, so— Never mind. She looked forward to seeing him tonight. It had been too long. And, besides, it was best to focus on other things for now, anyway.

If, for instance, there really was some connection between Hubert's disappearance and Shirley's death, as she was beginning to suspect— Well, she didn't need to investigate it, but at least she could put together all the pieces that she had. No more distractions.

At least the clear streets away from Main were boring enough to repel all but the most intrepid of tourists. Of course, the most intrepid were the ones whom she should have been trying hardest to avoid, and as she neared the end of Vico, a crowd of people in Refurserkir costumes turned the corner. Their fox-fur shirts made them seem more high-fashion than stealthy, but she had to admit that they looked surprisingly like the real thing.

They spotted her right away and moved as a group in her direction. She didn't notice the Gerd impersonator in the midst of them until they were already upon her, blocking the entire sidewalk so that she had no easy way of continuing onward.

"Hi. You probably want an autograph, right?"

The Gerd impersonator smiled. She, too, looked a lot like the real thing.

"We wouldn't want to trouble you," she said. Even her voice... Our Heroine squinted and looked a bit closer.

No. She seemed a little too young to be Gerd.

Unless she was just incredibly well preserved.

"That's a really nice costume," Our Heroine said. The woman was wearing a long black robe that seemed to suit Gerd's sense of style. "So, I guess you're supposed to be my arch-nemesis."

"I guess that is indeed what I am supposed to be. Yet we are in a hurry. No time to play at being nemeses now. I'm glad to have had the chance of seeing you, though." She smiled a genuinely friendly smile. It couldn't be Gerd.

"Yeah, well, have fun with all the dressing up and stuff," Our Heroine said, and she stepped onto the street around them all, not looking back as she turned the corner onto Telegraph—toward the campus.

She passed shops that catered to the student crowd: record stores, cafés, and copiers. It was early in the semester, and students were lining up to buy course readers, chugging lattes and hot apple ciders to compensate for the cold. Our Heroine considered a quick tea herself. Students might stop her, though, and she'd had enough conversation for the time being. She hurried on.

With cold feet she headed up Dalkey Road, where the wind seemed thicker. Away from downtown, from Hrothgar's, toward home. Perhaps Hubert would try to call again, and this time she'd find the phone. Screw him. She crossed the footbridge over Inwit Creek. Perhaps she'd refuse to answer.

So. It wasn't that she was searching, but she'd just ended up with these random pieces. Not of a puzzle, necessarily, but pieces of *something*. She had no surface on which to scribble this down. Just repeat it in her mind, then. Rearrange the fragments until they made sense.

Things that began with H: Hubert, *Historia Danica*, *Hamlet*—some versions, at least—Hrothgar's, Heidrun. Not now.

Things that she did not know: what Angus was doing in town tonight, whether that Nathan fellow had anything to do with all of this, whether there was a "this" to begin with...

Things that must be kept secret: what happened to Shirley in Denmark. Just the one thing, really. It had been the last thing that Shirley had asked of her—to keep it secret, particularly from Blaise. And if anyone deserved to know, it was he, so how could she tell anyone else? Besides, it might help but it might not. And if it were unrelated, then she would be betraying Shirley's trust for nothing. Better to honor her will than to get her an unasked-for revenge...

There were also things that she knew but could not say—things she had not yet found the voice to express.

Then she looked up at the sky and saw a column of black smoke. The color of Gerd's hair. More like a blaze than someone's chimney-flow. Black tree branching in the sky. At least it was a bit too far away to be from her house. But something was burning, and it was probably something that she didn't want burnt. She could feel sick already, imagining all the things it might be.

Skellington Road veered more directly toward home, but Our Heroine decided to continue down Dalkey. It was getting on toward two o'clock, and Bean Day pilgrims would be gathered round her house, and that was not something that she wanted to deal with. Though it might be worth braving through them just to get out of the cold... No. She could hear sirens, now, and curiosity tugged her hardest.

"Is my father all right?"

His library. The smoke had been coming from his library. The burning brought sensation back to the rims of her ears.

"Is my father all right?"

"I don't believe there was anyone inside, miss. Now you'll have to stand back."

Ash floated up out of it like negative snow.

"Oh, God, I have to find my father."

"I'm sorry, miss, I'm going to have to ask you to stand back for your own protection."

The fireman placed his smoke-smeared glove on her shoulder and led her back onto the street.

"Isn't there anyone who can tell me what's going on?"

"There's a fire, and I've got to go finish putting it out. I'm sorry that I can't assist you any more than that right now, but if you'll excuse me..."

The street around her was crowded with neighbors and tourists.

"I do not want this," she mumbled.

She imagined the books inside flaring one by one and her father in there with them.

"Pardon me, could I trouble you for an autograph?" spat a fat, graybearded fellow bumping abruptly up behind her.

"Now's not the time—"

"Oh, but please! Yours is the last I need."

She removed her eyes from the fire and frowned at the old man.

"Fine." She took his pad and scrawled her pseudonym illegibly upon it. She handed the pad back to the man, and he grinned maliciously up at her from behind his grey mass of beard and moustache.

"Thank you so much," he said as he wobbled off out of the crowd.

Our Heroine didn't notice her father until he grabbed her by the arms.

"This is the flame-work of Surt," Ymirson bellowed.

Smoke stung her eyes. "Papa! You're okay. Oh, we should get you to the hospital. Were you inside there? What happened? Did you inhale any smoke?"

"I have no need of a hospital, my dear. I have not been inhaling smoke, and I was not inside the blazing, either, so you should not be afraid for me." He was wearing his long brown heavy coat.

"How did this happen?"

"These are the flames of Surt."

Our Heroine saw the library reflected in her father's eyes. The firemen had reduced it almost to a smolder.

"Did you see someone start this fire, Pa?"

"We must catch him. That is all that is important. Then I may cry on my throne for having no more to do."

"I'm gonna take you back to my house, okay, Pa? You should lie down. We can talk to the fire department later. But let's just get out of here before they start asking questions."

"Yes, perhaps I should rest for the final fight that is yet to come." He straightened his spine to something like the full height he once had known. Still six feet, yet thinner and gray. It was no longer a tall six feet. He turned to walk with Our Heroine homeward.

"Are you sure you didn't try to work the oven by yourself or something, Pa? Do you remember anything about what happened? What were you doing when you realized the library was burning?"

"I don't know, dear thing. Do not ask me these questions right now. I am trying to think of what is to be done."

They walked without speaking. At least he was all right. More sirens sounded in the distance, Dopplering their direction. How did a fire start on such a snowy day? Just audible beneath the melody of the approaching engines, then, Our Heroine could discern a vague counterpoint. Somewhat familiar. Her eyelids opened wide when she recognized it as the howl of Garm.

"We're going to take a little detour, now, Pa."

ICELANDER

LUDO

NATHAN[24]

Despite the ceaseless sunlight of high summer, the air was bitter with the prevailing Arctic winds. My Vanatru guides seemed warm enough in their fox-fur parkas, but me, I was shivering like an idiot in the vintage Richard Roundtree black-leather jacket and brown turtleneck that I'd bought before leaving New Uruk. Three layers of thermals, too. This get-up had kept me feeling warm and looking cool in Denmark, Reykjavik, and all the way up to the northern coast,

24. The constant shifting between multiple narrators in this portion of the novel renders the chronology somewhat unclear, but internal evidence would suggest that the sections narrated by Nathan occur during the summer of 1998 while all other sections occur—like the rest of the text—on Bean Day of 2001 (except where explicitly noted otherwise). I was indoors for most of this day, myself, and thus unfortunately can offer little in the way of first-hand corroboration for any of this.

but honestly I almost would have skinned the horses if we hadn't had to leave them at the last outpost.

My guides were father and son. The son looked about my age, and I hit it off with him well enough. Told him stories about Hollywood, actors and actresses that I'd worked with—he mostly wanted to hear about the actresses. I just told him random shit about America, like how people hand you your change instead of setting it on the counter. But I felt that his father resented me somehow. Maybe it was just that he spoke no English, but he laid this silence on me like I'd done something so horrible he couldn't even yell at me about it. He hardly said anything to his son, either. Just a few sporadic barks, like "keep up," or "this way." Some sort of orders, I was sure.

"Don't worry about him," the son told me. "For three hundred dollars he likes you fine." Even so, the only acknowledgment he showed me at all was when I began to lag behind with my aching legs and he slackened his pace to brisk. I said thanks, but he just mumbled something to his son.

"What'd he say?" I asked.

"He says hurry up, tired legs are better than frozen ones. He says we'd have more energy to walk if we didn't talk so much."

A long silence followed. I started to feel like quiet was appropriate, though; the landscape looked quiet, the cold air smelled quiet. It almost made me forget how miserable I was with my moustache stuck to my face in frozen snot and my hands slipping into frostbit senselessness. I didn't think it was supposed to get this cold here, at least at this time of year. I was contemplating living the rest of my life without any fingers when the son tapped me on the shoulder and said, "This is it. We're there."

I looked around but couldn't see anything particularly notable.

"I was born here," the son told me. I ignored him and looked over at his father, who was lighting up a Marlboro that I could smell even through the snot-glacier in my nose. My last pack was still sitting on my bedside table in Reykjavik. I'd left it there out of some perverse idea I had about making my little pilgrimage in purity. It smelled like post-coital bliss, but I didn't want to bum one from him. At least I didn't want to ask. I coughed emphatically a few times, and he just looked at me and took a drag, holding the cigarette with both hands between fingers laced together in front of his mouth. I'd never seen anyone smoke that way before. It reminded me somehow of a documentary I'd seen about this sad old gorilla who'd never gotten used to life in the zoo. After a few quiet minutes while he finished his cigarette, I followed the two of them down the crater's steep incline.

God. I'd lost my only pair of contacts in a drunken stumble down the Strøget in Copenhagen—the less said about which the better—so maybe it was just my eyes. Or maybe it was the blood freezing in my brain, or just a trick of the steam rising up from the earth to tumble like a lover with the condensation in the frigid air... But the sky seemed suddenly to bend and shimmer around me as we approached the archway at the crater's bottom. Like in a movie when the hero passes through some invisible barrier into another dimension. The stink of sulphur got stronger. We were there. Beneath me I could feel the vulcanopneumatic power thrumming like

Brando's Triumph Thunderbird in *The Wild Ones*. I stared hard into the depths of the cave, standing still for a moment and trying to take it all in, and I swear I could already make out the vague green glow of the ormolu lichen within. The son's words no longer seemed so absurd to me. This was it. I was about to enter Vanaheim.

OUR HEROINE[25]

"This is not the way to Vanaheim," my father said as we made our way in the direction of Garm's howls.

"We'll be there soon, Pa. First we just have to make one little stop to pick up Garm."

"Hmph," he snorted. "This is nonsense. I have never shared your mother's fondness for hounds. We should leave for Vanaheim immediately."

WIBLE & PACHECO

Once he had parted from Our Heroine outside Hubert Jorgen's storefront, we proceeded to follow the actor for what seemed like minutes. The snow was useful in obscuring us from his sight, but perhaps we were not as obscure as we might have

---

25. Though Our Heroine otherwise seems to be the narrative focalizer of the novel as a whole, her first-person narration, here, seems relatively sparse in comparison to the more fully developed sections devoted to Nathan, Wible & Pacheco, and Blaise Duplain. While Part One (Prelude) appears to be perhaps an attempt to evoke the Valisonian voice while simultaneously resisting submission to the standard tropes of his more "mystery" oriented narratives, Part Two (Ludo) seems to set the reader adrift in a sea of narrators while Our Heroine struggles simply to find a voice that she can call her own.

been; it is possible that he was attempting to shake us from his trail. His path followed no pattern that we could perceive. Meanderings that crossed each other and doubled back upon themselves, like the aimless explorations of a man without a map in a city that he does not know. He seemed to be tracing out some indecipherable hieroglyph in the rough lines of the city streets. A rune of protection? From whom? We overtook him before he could achieve its terrible completion.

"Pardon us," we said as we caught him up. "May we speak with you for a moment?"

"Oh, hey..." Impassive. "Yeah, it's really me. So, do you guys want an autograph or something?" He patted at his pockets, presumably for a pen.

"There is no need for that; we are aware of your name. You are an actor as well as an author, are you not?"

With mute nod and sheepish smile, he affirmed our assertion.

"Hmm. It is a bit of an anomaly to find a celebrity of your caliber in a town as small as New Crúiskeen."

"Yeah, I'm just here for Bean Day, actually... I'm speaking at the Valison panel. And, if you guys don't want autographs, I should probably get a move on, because it starts pretty soon..."

"Of course. We do not mean to delay you... But my partner and I were just—quite coincidentally—discussing your superlative interpretation of the role of Hamlet, and we were hoping that, perhaps, you could spare just a moment to discuss it with us."

He was taken in by our subterfuge.

"You guys saw that? Yeah, I'm really proud of that movie.

I mean, I realize I'm no Olivier, but I do feel that it was one of my finer portrayals."

"Indeed. It was an astounding mimesis, and you must have studied the character in some depth to render it with such verisimilitude."

He mock-waved away our flattery.

"Yeah, well, I did take it pretty seriously," he said. "I'd never really done much Shakespeare before, so I spent a lot of time just reading the play—over and over—until I was sure I understood every single word... I even went to Denmark for a while, just to get a feel for the atmosphere in which it takes place, you know."

"Hmm..." we said, genuinely pensive, for this resonated unexpectedly well with other entries in our casebook. "During what period of time were you there, exactly?"

"Oh, that was back in the summer of '98. It took a couple years for the film to hit the States, and even then it didn't get a wide release... It was a good experience all around, though; I really learned a lot. I mean, for instance, did you know that Shakespeare wasn't even the first guy to write a story about the character? The early versions were more action-adventure than tragedy, apparently. But I was able to work a lot of that into my portrayal. If you ever watch the movie again, you should pay attention to how the way I develop as a character parallels way that the character evolved. From Saxo Grammaticus straight through to Thomas Kyd. And then Shakespeare, of course... I mean, it's pretty subtle, yeah, but it's all in there."

All of the fears that we had harbored till now—that the object of our search was but an *ignis fatuus*; that no true illumination awaited us at the end of our path; that we had been led on, thus far, by mere coincidence—had dissolved in the moment that the actor said the name. Thomas Kyd. Until our involvement with Ms. MacGuffin, we had been incognizant of this name, just as we had been incognizant of his purported *Hamlet*. Further, from what we knew of the actor, it did not seem likely to us that such information would ordinarily be found in the domain of his knowledge, either. We were excited, then, at the prospect of what seemed to be both confirmation of our fundamental hypotheses and an undeniable lead in new directions. We did not, however, allow this excitement to influence our tone of voice.

"Thomas Kyd?" we asked. "But Thomas Kyd's version of the play is lost, is it not?"

"Yeah, wow... Well, you guys are way more up on your *Hamlet* than I ever was. I'd never even heard of his version before I took on the role... But yeah, I guess it's lost, or it was never properly published or something. In Denmark, though, I met this woman who was trying to reconstruct it... Or at least she was trying to write her own verbally viable version of it or something. Like one that conformed to the syntactic patterns of Kyd's other plays. It sounded like a pretty cool idea..."

"This is all... quite intriguing," we said.

"Yeah... Well, anyway, it was nice talking to you guys..." he indicated his watch. "But I've really gotta be going."

"Indeed you do," we replied. "Indeed you do."

NATHAN

Feeling oozed back into my hands before we reached the bottom of the cave. The stench of sulphur was pretty strong, but if that meant warmth, then I figured I could get to like the smell pretty easily. About fifty meters down the tunnel, right around the first bend, there was a little kiosk where an ancient park ranger was sleeping with this huge grin on his face. The son walked up and knocked on the glass, but I was kind of sorry to see the old guy roused, he'd looked so happy. I imagined he was dreaming of a long-dead wife. Or maybe his wife was alive and he was dreaming of some girl he'd known before he got married. After he'd rubbed his eyes awake, he just gave us a tired frown.

"I'd like to get a three-day pass," I said.

The guy looked completely blank. Like he was blind from birth and I'd just asked him why the sky was blue. But there was no way he didn't speak English. Sure, most tourists enter Vanaheim at Snaefellsjökull—and that's exactly why I was entering here, to avoid the crowds—but I was pretty sure that even at this entrance they still got American tourists all the time. I considered trying my mediocre Danish out on him, but thought better of it when I remembered how well that had gone over in Denmark. The father stepped in to save me the embarrassment.

"Give my father your wallet," the son told me. "He will return you a fair remainder."

I handed it over—I had almost two hundred bucks in it, but what else was I gonna do—and the two older men began to yell at each other.

"It will be fine," the son said. "You just have to wait a couple of moments while they niggle over the price. Do you want a Royal Crown? I will buy it." He motioned toward a gift shop a couple decimeters beyond the kiosk.

"Yeah, okay."

We walked over together. There was no one inside except a teenage shopgirl reading some Icelandic cine-mag. I don't know how she managed to make out the words, because the only light came from the fluorescent green tubes lining the ceiling. An imitation of ormolu lichen, I guessed, though it felt more like a spaceship. I just hoped she didn't recognize me and start screaming and everything. Knowing my luck, I half-expected to see myself on the magazine's cover.

The son pulled two RC Colas from the refrigerator in the back.

"Do they have any Coke?" I asked.

"Royal Crown is the official soft drink of Vanaheim."

He was paying, so I figured I shouldn't argue. Then I recalled the reason why he was paying.

"Listen," I said, picking up some igneous rock that they were trying to sell as a souvenir. "Are you sure your dad and that old guy aren't gonna just split all my money between themselves?"

"The old man is a topsider. My father and I have no compassion for him or his kind. It shall only cost you sixty dollars, because my father will take great enthusiasm in niggling for you such that the oppressive topsider will obtain no extra money for himself. Of course, my father may extract a small fee for his passionate niggling."

"Of course."

The whole Vanaheimic hatred of topside Iceland was just totally strange to me. It was like the old episode of *Star Trek* where the black-and-white aliens hate the white-and-black aliens. I mean, the language was basically the same, the people all looked pretty similar, and they all lived on the same island, so I just didn't see what the problem was or why Vanaheim would even care about independence. Still, if it meant that the father would niggle extra hard on my behalf, I guessed I was all for it.

OUR HEROINE

I was so determined in rushing along, myself, that I almost failed to catch my father's hand when he stumbled stepping down from a curb. All of his books were burnt, I realized, like the neurons in his brain. When he straightened up and stretched himself to his full height, though, I saw him for a moment as he'd been *before*. Even with his waning mind, I could see him swell with the half-remembered ardor: his hatred of Surt, his love of my mother. His fury and pain when she died.

BLAISE

It is yesterday morning. I have just returned to my home, and I am receiving a call telling me that my wife is dead. What do I do?

How has it happened? Why has it happened? These are not the first thoughts that occur to me. I do not immediately become the investigator. First my face turns pink and bloated, and the red blood flows through the tendrils in my eyeballs. It is a time when I do not deny the water from my eyes.

I hear myself but I do not attend much to what I hear. I am trying to attract my attention, heaving and yelling, and hitting myself in the chest and head. There is more of this, and my hand is bleeding when I again take notice. I have broken the mirror at which my wife would fix her face, framed in tiny bulbs of light as if she were an actress. I turn on the bulbs and bandage my hand with gauze.

Still I do not begin to investigate. I lie on our bed with one of her fuzzy-collared coats upon my head and a large pillow between my legs and another in my arms to feel as if I am holding her. I desire to feel her move against me and to taste her bitter shampoo of which the pillow in my arms still smells. I wish to hear her making funny voices.

It is yesterday afternoon, and I am sitting on our bed with her journals around me and the few letters that she sent me from Denmark. Addressed: *My little cabbage.*

I am only eager for the shape of her words, and I think not of the meanings they enclose. If my ears cannot have her voice, then my eyes, though weeping, will have her writing. I feel my face contorted and try to hold it together between the covers of one of her journals, my nose pressed into the crack of spine. I do not smell anything. It is some time before I finally begin to read for meaning and, with great wretchedness, become the investigator.

WIBLE & PACHECO

After our encounter with the actor, we followed his trail backward to the source; for the second time that day, our investigation had led us to enter a private domain that was alien from our own. Now the librarian's store; earlier the home of Our Heroine. One space male, the other female. Opening the shop door, we considered the symmetry of the situation.

Within the store, we were confronted with the meaningless void of darkness. Climbing through Our Heroine's kitchen window, we had been confronted rather with a noise whose semiotic value was not so easily measured.

Question: Can the bark of a dog be said to "mean" anything? We might, for instance, have reasonably considered the yelps of the dachshund below the window to connote something like "Leave this place, intruders; you are not welcome within these walls." But the dachshund then being quieted with sausage links offered from our pockets, was it not also reasonable of us to revise our interpretation such that the same yelps were seen to have connoted something more akin to "Strangers, I demand tribute. My voice shall not be stifled until my belly is sated." Detached from context, the yelps can signify nothing; yet the silence in which they furiously resounded imbued them with more meaning than any response possibly could.

"Hello?" we called then through the gaping shop door.

A slight echo was the only response.

OUR HEROINE

The howls of Garm, though not far off, had already ceased when my father fell face-first into the snowbank of the sidewalk.

"Pa, are you all right?" I knelt beside him and tried to turn him over, but he wouldn't move.

"I am fine, dear thing." His words were muffled by the dirty snow. "There is nothing for you to worry about. Leave me be."

"I should have taken you to a hospital."

"No, no. I need no hospital. I will have no such thing."

"I need to turn you over, Pa."

"The snow is cold. It is like clumsy whiteness numbing my face."

"That's why I need to turn you over."

I attempted to roll him again, and this time he allowed me.

"I saw his face," he sputtered, blowing snow from his lips. I wiped more from his eyes. "Yes, yes, thank you, that is fine. I saw the face of Surt, dear thing, despite much snow in my eyes and my vision blurred."

"..."

"Emily was there also. She was in danger. We must find her without delay."

"Oh, Pa, how did you get so bad all of the sudden?"

He snorted derisively. "It is not I who am bad, dear thing. Surt is the bad one, as always. But we have wasted too much time in dallying here while he has time to disguise his handiwork. Let us go."

He started to get up and I helped him the rest of the way. "All right, Pa, we're just going to pick up Garm, then we'll all head home and plan the next step from there, all right?"

"Hmm... Yes, that sounds like a reasonable plan."

"Hey there, strangers!" At the end of the block Constance Lingus was yelling in our direction.

BLAISE

It is this morning and I have been awake all night, breaking more things and screaming in the empty and otherwise silent bedroom unfilled with Shirley's snores. I have been scratching at scrawled-over words in Shirley's journals and musing on the missing pages. My fingernails are blue and my eyes are red. Overheated coffee has numbed my tongue, but I say her name.

She called her coffee "phlogiston."

I am a fish. This the central line from the Two-Story House,[26] I know, but what is it doing here amongst her notes on Denmark? What happened there?

Sometimes I really want to XXXXXXXXXXXXXXXX *{illegible/scrawled-over}.*

There is much that I do not understand.

All my words shall be stallion, not a workhorse among them.

We must create incomprehensible things in order to have an analogy for our incomprehension of the universe. Obscure reality to make it more attractive. We must keep secrets, so that others may have the pleasure of uncovering them: wow.

She succeeded in creating many incomprehensible things.

NATHAN

Trying to chat with the shopgirl while the son was off taking a piss and the father was still busy "niggling," I suddenly realized just how strange it was to be in a place where I couldn't understand the local language and no one would speak to me in English, so I just shut up and headed outside. The father was already standing outside the shop door, smoking another cigarette. This time I didn't even bother to hint that I wanted one.

The son took his time, but eventually he came out, and

---

26. One of the only extant pieces of Shirley MacGuffin's fiction. More on this later.

I followed him and his dad through the turnstiles and down a long unlit tunnel. And then we entered the first major cavern, which—according to my guidebook—was known as the Hall of Foxes.

YMIRSON

I have never had much fondness for hounds. When I was a young boy I had a hound. He would often chew things that I did not want him to chew, and though it was I who answered for his crimes, he refused to learn from my instruction. I had but a small fondness for him.

My wife has a fondness for hounds. This increases my ill feeling toward the creatures, for I am selfish and Emily's fondness could be devoted all the more strongly to me were she to refuse it to them. I have told her this often. Though it was a hound that first brought me to my Emily. The Fenris Dachshund is a good hound, as hounds go. I do not always object when he licks my face. Hounds have their place in this world, but that place is mostly not within my fondness.

BLAISE

Every dog has his day, and a bad dog might have two.

It is last night and I am reading Shirley's journals for the first time since her death.

She kept no record of dates. Her habit was to open journals at random and write her words wherever her pen first found empty space. This renders her story difficult to follow. It was her pleasure to be cryptic.

I can't tell Blaise about this.

What cur was this of which she could not tell me? What deed was it for which Shirley deemed him a "bad dog"?

The portions of the journal which aspire to relate particular events tell me very little. Her shorthand was overly honed.

Clement weather, meeting tonight, café with bad Turkish phlogiston. Ugh. Consistency like: mud? K. Order something else. Or at least know next time not to drink the dregs.

But I know my wife better than this. The surface of these entries is not where her story is to be read. I know her tricks, for she was always too eager to explain them to me. I see from this last fragment, for instance, that I was the cuckoo—what happened in Denmark?—and I begin the journals yet again with this new view in my mind.

OUR HEROINE

"It's good to see you," Constance Lingus said as we met her halfway down the block. She looked a bit ridiculous with her short ginger hair and puffy red jacket framing her cold-flushed freckled face. "I figured you wouldn't be far from your dog."

"Where!" I grabbed her and my father each by an arm and dragged them back in the direction from which she'd come.

"Well, what is the *cause d'aventure* today, then?"

"I'm just looking for my dog."

"I am only too delighted to show you the way to your missing pup, but I thought that perhaps you could be enticed to answer a few— No need to pinch, now! I can better lead the way if you unhand me."

"Sorry... I've been worried about him all morning, though.

I just want to make sure he's okay."

She rubbed her arm over-dramatically where I'd been holding her. "Well, you need worry no more. He looked to be having a very good time, bounding through the snow in pursuit of some canine companion. I hesitantly suggest that we can safely slow to a saunter without endangering his life."

"I don't want to lose him."

Constance murmured something snide to which I chose not to reply.

"Addressing Mr. Ymirson, now," she continued, "I wanted to tell you that I overheard the police call about your library. I'd been on my way there to make sure that no one had fallen in the way of harm when I happened across first your dog and then the two of you. As we head away from the fire, might I ask if its source has been determined yet?"

"They haven't told us anything official," I answered.

"The police call didn't say anything about any injuries, at least. Or deaths... I suppose you've heard about Shirley?"

"I got the call yesterday."

"I should mention that I'm covering the story... An interview—"

"She is that dread reporter, dear thing. Do not answer her questions."

"Sorry, Connie, but I'm going to have to bow to my father's wishes on this one."

NATHAN

The father and son were leading the way, and the passage was pretty narrow, so I didn't get any preview of the Hall of Foxes until I'd already entered it. Once I saw it, though, it just sucked the breath right out of my lungs. I'd been expecting something like the underground cities of Turkey—cramped passageways connecting the relatively few rooms that you could actually stand in. But not even the Catacombs of Alexandria could have prepared me for this.

The cavern must have been about thirty meters high, which was odd since I didn't think we'd descended that far. The walls formed a rough pentagon, and scenes from Vanatru mythology were carved all over them. I recognized a few of the images, like Frey's death in the autumn and his resurrection in the spring, but most of the significance was lost on me.

Natural pillars of shiny, black volcanic rock held up the ceiling, which was blanketed in ormolu lichen. The neon tubes back in the shop had led me to expect something more glaring and sickly, but the glow of the real thing was gentle. Organic, and warm like steam. The look of it, like the green sky before a Midwestern thunderstorm,[27] almost made me forget I was underground.

The locals had set up a few booths along the main avenue through the cavern. They were mostly just hawking the usual souvenirs—fake wooden idols and fox figurines, some dried bits of ormolu lichen—but next to one of the booths there was a dirty little black-haired kid selling these glossy four-colored maps. Somehow I'd thought everyone here would look stereotypically

---

27. The Master's description of a similar scene in *The Fox in the Snow* (*The Memoirs of Emily Bean* Vol. 4) as "the light of a green sun whose orb was diffused across the entirety of the sky" takes into literary account the fact that the primary deity of the Vanatru religion is Frey—a sun god—and not the more popular thunder god apparently favored by the author of the current narrative.

Nordic, but—based on the people I'd seen so far—most of the Vanatru were smaller and darker than my expectations. The kid was wearing a shirt that read "Adodis" and had a subtle knock-off of an Adidas logo on it. Something about that just cracked me up, so I asked him how much the maps were.

"You won't need that," the son told me.

I bought one anyway, though, and then we headed down the avenue.

Once we'd gotten a little beyond the main cavern, the avenue walls bottlenecked together. Like that narrow canyon that Harrison Ford goes through in *Indiana Jones* before he finds the Grail Castle. Now that we were in the son's territory, I suddenly noticed there was no more talk of Hollywood.

"The Treasury is probably Vanaheim's best-known feature," he told me as we slowed to a mosey, trapped behind a group of old tourists in the bottle-neck. "It's the first big attraction a man sees when he enters at Snaefellsjökull. An artist's representation of it is used on the front cover of Magnus Valison's *The Fox in the Snow*."

"Yeah, I read that. So, the Treasury's the one with the big building face carved directly into the stone, right? All decorated with spears and shields and stuff? It looked pretty impressive on the book cover..."

"Yes, that is it, but the first big attraction that we will show you is impressive even more so." Just as he said this, the avenue opened up to another big cavern. "This is the temple of the Refurserkir."

Refurserkur literally means something like "fox-shirter," and on the map that I'd bought the temple before me was marked with a little cartoon fox head. Cameras aren't allowed in Vanaheim, but even if I'd had one, it couldn't have done justice to the real thing.

The tourists in front of us were gawking in awe.

The front of the temple was actually shaped like a gigantic fox head, carved out of one big mass of rock. I couldn't believe the detail of the thing, and on such a massive scale.

"Now why isn't this called the Hall of Foxes?" I asked.

"Because this is the Hall of the Fox-Shirters," the son answered me. "The men become fox. This is we. My father and I. We are Refurserkir."

"Really?" I pulled my eyes away from the temple to see if he was joking. "I thought the Refurserkir were like ninjas or something."

"We are like foxes that are full of tricks and stealth. That is why we wear the fur of foxes."

"You're kidding, right? I mean, don't take this as an insult, but the two of you don't seem particularly sneaky to me."

"Of course we have other clothes for when we must be sneakier. These clothes are more for the resilience of the fox to cold."

"Huh. I just thought you guys would be more imposing."

"Like the fox, we are not so imposing to look at, but we—"

I don't know if the father understood what was being said or if he just didn't like the amount of talking going on in general, but he suddenly smacked the son on the back of the head and grumbled something at him in Vanaheimic.

The son rubbed where his father had hit him. "All right... It is true. We in actuality are only servants of the Refurserkir. But we are trained in their ways. Trust that we could impose you if such imposition were to become necessary."

"Well, show me a trick or something."

"Okay. Watch this." He started to reach inside his parka.

I can't say exactly how it happened, then—it was all kind of blurry—but the next thing I knew, the father had somehow spun around and thrown the son to the ground. And the son just lay there for a minute.

"Maybe I should not show you any tricks after all," he said, eventually, accepting my hand to help him to his feet.

"Yeah, cool..." I said. "Can I go inside the temple, though?"

WIBLE & PACHECO

Though Our Heroine and the actor (whose words remained bright in our minds) had left the door unlocked, it seemed that no one else had infiltrated the interior of the librarian's store. We were, to all appearances, alone. As the store was still immersed in its opaque bath of shadows, however, the accuracy of all appearances was difficult to ascertain. We treaded, therefore, carefully to the switchbox in back—neither fools nor angels—and dispelled the darkness.

Newly illuminated in the light of halogen, the amount of potential information with which we were faced overwhelmed us. Our Heroine had led us here, and we were thus confident that none of the books here shelved could fail to yield some relevant information concerning the case—just as no shell can fail to speak of the ocean or of the various species of oceanic mollusk-hunting fauna. Yet the cost in time of extracting the information must be balanced against the information's value. Such equations were not easy to calculate on the basis of covers alone, however, and consequently it would not be a simple matter to narrow our search.

We walked the aisles of the store, then, with eyes open for the incongruous. The truly antique books in their glass display cases were kept separate from the merely rare, yet—other than this—the system according to which the store was arranged remained inscrutable to us. The traditional practice of organization in reference to author's surname had seemingly been eschewed in favor of a method far more arcane.

This raised the question: How does one locate the incongruous in a system that emulates chaos? In the general semblance of maelstrom, what order was there from which to deviate? Most of the volumes possessed no commonalities save those of age and scarcity. On any given shelf, only the loosest of thematic or biographical ties bound together two adjacent tomes.

So engrossed were we in our search that we did not perceive the opening and closing of the store's front door. Unless he'd already been there before we arrived... We heard him speak before we saw him.

"Egad! You fellows nearly frightened the dickens out of me!"

It took us a moment to recognize this nondescript man with his thin gray hair and thin gray suit; we stood quietly appraising him for a moment before his ridiculous phraseology and the leather valise clutched to his side reminded us of his identity.

"You are the literary agent. Philip Leshio. You represent Magnus Valison. And you also represented Shirley MacGuffin, before she died."

"Right ho." He grinned at us maliciously. "And you're those chaps who made such a botch of the Bean-Ymirsons's L'anse aux Meadows[28] case, yes?"

"If that is how you choose to remember it."

"Yes, so. Is Jorgen anywhere to be found? I have two books right here that I think he'd be greatly interested in." He patted his valise as he spoke.

"He is not on the premises, to our knowledge."

"Ah. Well, I'll just toddle off then. Valedictions!"

"You are in town for Ms. MacGuffin's funeral, we assume."

He paused on his way toward the door. "Is this to do with her murder? She never earned me a single schilling, that girl, with her houses and *Hamlet*s and scribblings in the sand, but I always had a special place in my heart for her."

"Yes, she shall be missed. We knew her only slightly, though we were enthusiasts of her works. Indeed, we look forward to reading her *Hamlet*, if ever you secure a publisher."

"If you refer to the preposterous Thomas Kyd emulation that she was working on, I'm afraid you'll be waiting a rather longish time. I don't believe she ever quite finished it. And even had she done so, I don't suppose I could find a publisher for it."

"Indeed?" we asked.

"Yes, indeed," he answered. "For one thing, who—besides, apparently, the two of you—would be enticed by the prospect of a perfect imitation of a minor sixteenth-century playwright? Few enough read the Bard, these days, and all the fewer Kyd."

---

28. L'anse aux Meadows is the site of an early Viking settlement in Newfoundland from circa 1000 A.D. The details of the strange crimes that occurred there in 1980 can be found in *Would as Leif*, the aforementioned seventh volume of Valison's *The Memoirs of Emily Bean.*

"We see. Yet—"

"And, for another thing, there are simply far too many overzealous Shakespeareans in the world, and I'm afraid most of them would take her play as nothing less than a straight up 'Nuts to you!' She actually had the audacity to include some of the true *Hamlet*'s most memorable moments, nigh verbatim, in her version. Polonius's speech to Laertes, the gravedigger scene... The upshot being, of course, that Shakespeare's greatest play was little more than a polite knock off of Kyd. I found the suggestion a trifle insulting myself, and I am not of a particularly sensitive temperament, I assure you."

"We see. Though no one would find it a sufficient insult to commit murder over, we trust."

"Oh, of course not. It was just a *hypothetical* reconstruction, after all... But I don't suppose we should really be hanging about here without him like this, now, should we? So, shall we leave?"

"Feel free." We escorted him to the door. "But we shall linger for a time."

"Hmph. Well, if you require any further assistance with the investigation—"

"You have assisted us enough," we told him.

He hesitated at the door, but stepped finally across the threshold when Mr. Pacheco harrumphed with peculiar zeal. We locked the door behind him before he could say anything further, then, and we turned to resume our search.

NATHAN

The son hesitated a moment and cast a glance at his father as he considered my request to be allowed inside the temple.

"It is a sacred place to the Refurserkir," he said. "Only a few outsiders have ever seen its inner chambers."

"Well, maybe I could just see its outer chambers."

He said something to his father, who paused before nodding.

"We will see what we can do," the son told me. "My father apparently is fond of you."

That was a little hard to believe, but I followed the two of them up to the entrance anyway. A middle-aged guard playing with a Swiss Army Knife and dressed in clothing similar to theirs stopped us as we approached. He spoke to the father while I just stood there admiring my shoes for fear of looking too lustingly at the doorway. I was down to my aglets when they stopped and the son finally spoke to me.

"My father wants you to know that he believes you to have the heart of a Refurserkur, or we would not be doing this. After much passionate niggling with the guard on your behalf, he has determined that you may enter. But the temple is in need of constant upkeep, and the guard has many children—"

"Okay, how much?" I asked.

"Sixty American dollars."

I pulled out my wallet; there was eighty dollars left in it.

"All right, here you go." I handed the money over. "But there better not be any other tourists in here who have the hearts of Refurserkir," I mumbled, "or I'm gonna want my money back."

BLAISE

Shirley always mumbled her meaning beneath shouts of misdirection. Like legerdemain, but sleight of words. By way of example, a representative salutation from one of her letters:

Lisp and stutter; bless your throat. My aim is true.

The first sentence is clear enough. It is a variation on one of her common greetings to me. Saint Blaise once prevented a man from choking to death on a fishbone and has since been regarded as the patron of healthy throats. "Bless" shares consonance with my name, which itself signifies a defect of speech, such as a stutter or particularly a lisp.

"Aim," however, is more complex. Sensitive to my native language, she implies the truth of her love, though *aimer* indicates something more familial than the feelings of passion which we shared. "Adore" is the cognate that she should have sought, unless this "truth" was in reference to her love for someone other than me. Yet she was fond of stratifying her words with as many meanings as possible. "Aim" could also here mean simply "direction" or "purpose." Perhaps, fully expanded, the sentence stands for something like "My purpose is noble and I mean not to misdirect you, only to express the purity of my love." Unless I have missed the point entirely. Her text is rich with such ambiguities.

It is this morning and I have laid her journals aside. I must mull the ambiguities. I rub my eyelids with the corns of my palms, but my tear ducts are drained. Pots of coffee have not helped to maintain my store of fluids. I move somehow from the bedroom to the kitchen to brew another pot. Perhaps I should change to tea.

My wife is dead. Light shines into the kitchen from the snow outside and then reflects off of the knife-scratched metal of our countertops. Through the window I stare for a moment at the Two-Story House in our backyard. It was built shortly before Shirley's departure to Denmark in the summer of 1998, though Shirley only finished the text after her return. The stories each had something to do with fish. I run the tap for a glass of water to replenish my fluids, but as the tumbler fills I realize that I am not thirsty for water after all. I am angry at my wife.

The percolator splutters its last liquid into the pot, and I pour some into the tumbler. It burns my hand to hold, but I am angry at myself for being angry at my wife. How can I be angry at her when she is dead? I believe that I know something of what happened while she was in Denmark. I sit in my chair at our small wooden table and place my coffee in front of me, attempting to drain it of heat with both of my hands. I do not use a coaster. Shirley would have been angry about this.

Sometimes I really want to XXXXXXXXXXXXXXXXX.

There are words that I cannot reclaim. They are buried beneath overlayings of ink that press beyond their roots, almost through to the other side of the page; they remain unrevealed by the most fervent scratching of my fingernails. There are pages that have been carefully sliced away with razors, their erstwhile existence betrayed only by the twins of leaf from which they have been severed. But these muted words speak almost as volubly as her cryptic mutterings. They speak of something that even her usually sufficient literary obfuscations could not serve to hide.

I finish my coffee quickly. I am not tired, but I must ensure my wakefulness. Close reading is not to be the only aspect of my investigation. Through the window I see the snow falling to cover our backyard. *His teeth were white as snow.* It has fallen like this all through the night and morning. But the morning grows old, and I have agreed to meet Our Heroine at the Elite Café in less than an hour. Shirley met with her often after returning from Denmark. Supposedly for the purpose of mutual literary critique. My hope, however, is that Shirley shared details with her that could only be shared with another woman. I shall see.

OUR HEROINE

The park came into view at the end of the road as Connie led the way. A grove of birch cluttered the close edge, rising white and brown out of the ground like extensions of the dirty snow, but between the trunks sledders could be seen slogging up and sliding down the slope of the far end. Garm wasn't evident anywhere in the area.

"Where is he?" I asked.

"This was where I saw him, down there, running right across the valley trough. I couldn't even offer a guess of where he's got to. It suddenly occurs to me, though... Do you suppose that the fire could have had anything to do with Shirley's death? Perhaps the killer torched the library?"

"Now's not the time, Connie."

I held onto my father's arm as we descended into the park's bowl.

"I know this place," he said as we approached the bottom. I should have taken him back to the house.

"That looks like the spot where I saw him." Constance pointed to a vague trail of disturbed snow leading from near where we stood up to the edge of park that bordered downtown.

"Item," she said, waving her hand in the air in front of

her. "Not-so-famed pup of the Bean-Ymirson clan gone missing just days after death of close family friend. Is there a connection? If not, why does Our Heroine seem so much more preoccupied with finding said canine than with the brutal murder of—"

"Something can still be done about Garm, Connie. I can find him. I can't save Shirley."

"I'm not talking about saving her. I'm talking about showing some emotion over the death of your friend. Remember the lesson of QE2 and the death of Di. Public befuddled over Our Heroine's apparent lack of concern."

"I don't care about the public, Connie. And you'd better not quote me on that. But I'm just not a public person, all right?" Sledders were beginning to notice us, now, which belied my statement just a bit.

"It seems to me that you just don't know how to mourn her," Connie said. "Faced with a meaningful death after a lifetime of conveniently forgettable corpses, Our Heroine—"

"Enough already. I haven't forgotten a single one of the people who've died in my life."

She was looking down at the ground, now. "I'm sorry. I didn't mean to imply that your mom—"

"Let's just drop it, " I sighed. "Garm's not here. But I'm worrying about this too much. He'll probably just find his own way home, anyway."

"The same old plan," she muttered. "Just let him run free for a bit and maybe he'll come back to you. And that theory has worked quite well in the past, hasn't it?"

"What?" I asked, sincerely unsure of what she'd said.

"I assure you, I'm only trying to— Is your father all right?"

"What does my father have to do with it?"

"Well, he's lying face-down in the snow behind you, there. I can't say what that has to do with your personal problems regarding Prescott and/or promiscuity, but it seems, to me, a pressing issue for him."

"Oh, God," I said, turning around. "Pa, why are you doing this?"

He murmured something into the snow that I couldn't comprehend.

"We have to get him indoors," I told Connie.

"We're going to help you up, Mr. Ymirson." She said it as if she were speaking to a child. "If that's all right with you, that is. You're going to have to work with us on this, though, as you're still a rather well-built man and I doubt that we two mere females could lift you on our own. Are you ready?"

"Yes, yes," he said. "I do not object."

We pulled him to his feet and each took an arm.

Constance looked across my father's back at me and gave a resigned sigh. "Of course I know that this is all confidential. I'm surprised that you would even suggest otherwise. You know I've always put our friendship before my professional interests."

"I just want you to promise me you won't print any of this. I want you to say it."

"Not a whit of what I've seen nor even what you've said shall see print, I promise. Now let's get your father home."

WIBLE & PACHECO

The only anomaly we were able to find in the store proper rested between an early printing of Herman Melville's *The Confidence*

Man and a first edition of Sir Arthur Conan Doyle's *Valley of Fear*.[29] In a store devoted to rare and antiquarian books there glistened brightly out of place a shiny, new paperback copy of Magnus Valison's *The Case of the Consternated Cossacks*. Lacking age, scarcity, and value, there was no reason that it should have taken space on any shelf of this store. Furthermore, we ourselves were featured as characters therein. We thus hypothesized that this book might provide us some clue as to what precise connection Our Heroine had to the librarian, Hubert Jorgen—and, more significantly, what connection he might have to the missing manuscript of Shirley MacGuffin.

Mr. Pacheco had read the book upon its initial release, and a brief perusal was enough to reacquaint him with its major themes and leitmotifs. The plot concerned restaurateurs, Refurserkir, Surt's hatred for imperialism in general and Denmark in particular, forgery, memory: cultural and personal, and the usual attempts of the Bean-Ymirson clan to bring everything to a tidy and just resolution. What relevance this had to the death of Shirley MacGuffin or to her *Hamlet* project, we could not yet guess with any certainty. The forgery theme was evocative, however. Jorgen was an expert on the subject. Perhaps someone wished to pass Ms. MacGuffin's approximation of Kyd off as the real thing. Or, conversely, per-

29. Considering Hubert Jorgen's status as the most ingenious library scientist of modern times, all facets of his organizational style should have been recorded in detail. Though horizontally the book may have been found between the two volumes mentioned, perhaps more relevant information might have been revealed if the investigators had taken note of the fact that the book's vertical neighbors were, say, Vladimir Nabokov and Elizabeth Peters. Not that I have any way of knowing. As it is, one can only speculate what valuable data was lost in their clumsy account.

haps someone wished to ensure that none would ever have the chance of mistaking it for the real thing.

Yet these were only hypotheses, and more information was required before we could either validate or refute them. Certain pages of the book we had found were dog-eared, and an almost illegible word was scrawled on the book's title page. Perhaps "Amleth." It did not appear to be Magnus Valison's signature, at least, and so we tentatively assumed it to be the name of the volume's previous owner. We resolved to study this in greater detail when time permitted, however. For the moment, Mr. Wible slipped the book into a plastic bag and stowed it safely in his leather satchel.

A final tour of the shop floor revealed no further anomalies, and in the interest of utilizing our time to its fullest value—the deepest mysteries being most often secreted in the innermost chambers—we decided to remove our search to the back room. The key was kept, predictably enough, in a drawer beneath the store's cash register, and a piece of plastic molded in the shape of an Arctic fox was attached to the keychain. The connection between this animal and the Refurserkir did not escape our attention, and the memory of our first encounter with those furtive beings was full in our minds as we opened the door and entered the darkness beyond.

NATHAN

What I could make out of the darkened interior of the Refurserkir temple was a lot plainer than I'd expected. No lichen grew within, and the father only had a little hand-pumped flashlight like they use in bomb shelters in all those Cold War movies. The dim pulse didn't shine coherently for any more than a meter in front of us, though, and all it revealed was dirty ground and bare gray walls. I had to keep my hand to the surface, and still the occasional cross-paths made me stumble a few times. The stone felt more like plastic than rock. We mostly followed the main tunnel spiraling inward.

"These walls are amazing," I said.

"They were not made by human hands," the son told me, his silhouette changing shape as he turned his head. "Before Vanaheim was settled, trolls lived here. The Refurserkir hired a troll to build this temple."

"You really believe that?"

"It is the story I was told when growing up. When the troll came for his payment, the Refurserkir denied him, so he cursed the temple to darkness. This is why no ormolu grows here. The troll demanded his payment again after this, but the Refurserkir discovered his name, and he became a part of the stone when they said it aloud. There is a place within here where you can see his face in the wall."

"Wait, he turned to stone just because somebody said his name? That's a pretty big weakness. I mean, how did anyone ever get his attention?"

"Names are powerful things. They are not to be given lightly."

"Well, what was this troll's name?"

"Sometimes he is called Short-Legs, but that is not his name. His name is a secret of the Refurserkir."

"I see." I let out an emphatic cough. "So, why didn't the

Refurserkir just pay him for his services in the first place, since he built the temple so well?"

"He was a troll... But you must not ask so many questions about our lore."

His silhouette seemed genuinely upset.

"Hey, I didn't mean to offend you," I said, after a few minutes of silence.

He didn't say anything for another minute, though his father, leading the way, hadn't seemed to mind our talking for once.

"I think he was a tricky troll," the son finally offered. "He probably tricked the Refurserkir into agreeing to an unfair price. So they had to refuse him his payment."

I wanted to argue, but I figured I'd better just make peace. "Yeah, that makes sense."

Eventually, after another silent minute or so of I don't know how many left turns, the tunnel opened into a large chamber lit with halogen tubes set in fixtures in the ceiling. An old man and a young woman were sitting on wooden chairs in the far corner, and a bunch of guys dressed in fox fur were hunched about the rest of the room chattering with each other in their weird lilting language. The center of the room was dominated by a big stone lectern.

"This is the Thing Room," the son told me. "It is where we meet to discuss things."

"Are these guys the Refurserkir?" I whispered.

"They... No. They are servants. Like I and my father."

"So, where are all the Refurserkir? This is their temple, isn't it?"

"This is the Temple of the Refurserkir. They are all

around us, though you do not see them. In the shadows, silent but deadly. Invisible like the wind, but even more silent than that."

This sounded like bullshit to me, and I'm the bullshit king, but I didn't say anything. The sulphur smell was stronger here than it had been outside, and it was more humid, too. I figured that there must be a steam pool somewhere. Without saying anything, the father went over and squatted with a group of the other servants.

"You wait here," the son told me, and he went and squatted, too.

I guessed that meant we were staying for a while.

OUR HEROINE

"I guess I'd better stay here with my dad," I said, coming down from the bedroom where I'd tucked my father in to the living room where Connie was waiting for me. "Garm will have to wait."

"Was that Dr. Albertine on the phone? Would it be beyond my place to ask what he said?" Constance asked.

"Not to worry, and that it was probably just stress. But I have to bring Pa in tomorrow afternoon. For now I'm just supposed to give him his medicine and let him get some rest... Thanks again for helping me bring him home."

"I'm always ready to lend my assistance when needed. If there's any other help I may offer, you've only to mention it."

She was sitting on the couch with her legs curled beneath her. She'd removed her shoes in the mudroom so as not to track in snow. I sat down in a chair across the coffee table from her.

Her smile was wide and she kept contact with my eyes.

"Look, Connie, I'm not sure what you think you're doing here, and I really am grateful to you for helping me out, but if this is about an interview, or in any way connected to Shirley's death—"

"Of course not! I'm only here to help you, I assure you. And I do believe you could use my help." The wood-burning stove was beginning to warm the place, but her face was still flushed with cold. She'd had no sweater on beneath her coat.

"Well, if this is about Prescott, then... Thank you, but I'm fine. It's been six months, and I don't need a shoulder to cry on or any of that—"

"Naturally. I wouldn't presume. Especially as you've a seeming surfeit of men with whom to drown whatever sorrows you might be suffering. Besides which, by my understanding of things the entire situation was your fault, so I'd be hard pressed to lend a sympathetic shoulder for your tears, even were you to want one."

"What?"

"I'm only here to—"

"What do you mean it was all my fault? What do you know about it, anyway? Where do—"

"Perhaps I've said too much. But I only meant that I spoke with Prescott shortly after his decision to leave, and—from his version of the story—it seemed quite clear who the guilty party was."

I began to rant. "Oh, so he couldn't explain himself to me, but he could go talk to you about the whole thing, and you don't see a problem with that? I mean, that doesn't signal to you that there was a fundamental lack of communication in our relationship, on his part, and that rather than talk to me, his wife, about whatever problems he had, he went off and confided in *you*. I mean, you don't see that as possibly symptomatic of the fact that there was a larger set of issues than whatever watered-down story he fed you? That maybe it wasn't a case of guilty versus innocent, but that perhaps it was just a bit more complicated than that?"

"I feel the flush of heated discussion in my cheeks. Now we're getting somewhere. But considering everything Prescott told me, it seems entirely appropriate that he confided in me without a word to you. After all, his decision to leave was directly set off by the fact that he caught you in the act of achieving... conversational catharsis, with Magnus Valison. I think Prescott was particularly hurt by the fact that you specifically mentioned that you could never have such a conversation with *him*."

"He— First off, we were talking about writing, and I *couldn't* have such a conversation with—"

"..."

"I mean, you make it sound as if I'd been having really boring phone sex."

"And so I intended. Prescott's precise concern was that you didn't find him intellectually sexy."

"He did not say 'intellectually sexy.'"

"Ah, but he did, I assure you. I imagine he fancied it an intellectually sexy way of saying 'smart.'"

"I can't— I do not want to talk about this. Especially not with you. I told you earlier that I don't want to talk about it, and I stand by that; I don't."

"Fine. That's not why I'm here."

"Then just why exactly *are* you here? You don't want an

interview, and you don't want to badger me about my personal life. So..."

She sighed resignedly. "I'm only here because I can help you. I have to type up some of my notes... And I think it would be a convenient solution for both of us if I were to do my work here—on your computer—and watch over your father for you while you go out and search for Garm."

"I— Well—"

Garm, Hubert; it would be better if I were at least out searching. Trying *something*.

"Well, I do have a typewriter you could use..." I said.

"Perfect. And I apologize if you inferred any insult from my professed desire to help you, but sincerely this is all I ever meant."

WIBLE & PACHECO

Propositions: Meaning must be arrived at obliquely, through hints and feints. It must be suggested through the figurative rather than explicitly stated through the literal. Any attempt to capture meaning by direct approach will result in its death, and—like certain shellfish—meaning must not be killed prior to ingestion lest it be rendered poisonous or, at the least, unpalatable. Meanings that can be contained in words are not worth discussing. Nothing need be passed over in silence, yet some things may be merely implied through circumlocution. Absence as a defining characteristic. Subjects defined by negative space.

All of this occurred to us as we groped futilely in the darkness for some source of illumination. Illumination came only too late, however—after Mr. Pacheco had already scattered a pile of books over the floor with his clumsy stumbling and landed on his knees beside them—and it came from an entirely unexpected source. While Mr. Wible manically slapped the wall in search of a switch, Mr. Pacheco produced a large metallic flashlight from beneath the workbench beside which he had fallen. Of course, if Mr. Wible had packed his own flashlight, which Mr. Pacheco had reminded him to do before they left—

The activated flashlight resolved the enigma of the nonexistent switch; the overhead bulb—had it not been broken—would have been operated, rather, by means of a chain that hung from a fixture in the ceiling. Mr. Pacheco pulled the chain to no effect as Mr. Wible retrieved a piece of the shattered bulb from the book-scattered floor. Mr. Wible examined this object for a moment before restoring it to its initial position beside a nineteenth-century edition of *Tristram Shandy*. Six feet away, a ladder led upward. We ascended.

The room above did not hold anything of much significance. More piles of books, a desk at the far end, and a window painted black. The books bore no features worthy of commentary. Upon the periphery of the desk rested a rotary phone, a lamp, and an amber jar of adhesive (whether for bookbindery or more recreational purposes, we dared not assume). The center of the desk's surface was occupied only by two conspicuously dustless rectangles of differing size, which attracted our attention precisely because we had no way of ascertaining what had so recently resided atop them.[30]

The most obvious answer was "two books," which called

30. This is the first of three semi-significant absences that I have located in the text (though there may be others that I have missed). I suspect that this one in particular is merely meant to make me wonder what happened to those supposedly precious pages.

to mind Leshio's comment that he had "two books" that he thought Jorgen would be greatly interested in. Would Jorgen not be interested in books taken from his own back room? And if Leshio had been in the store before us... But this line of thought was leading us too far into the realm of baseless postulation. The rectangles of absence were our only real data, and they in themselves provided us but little ground for hypothesis.

The window, by the very obscurity of its import, was also immediately compelling to us. Though the practical purpose of the black paint was apparent—direct sunlight damaged books—the extended symbolic implications were what intrigued us. Again, however, with no evidence on which to support one given interpretation over any other, we decided to reserve our speculation for the moment.

There was nothing more for us here.

So we returned to the shop floor, leaving the flashlight where we had found it. Where Mr. Pacheco had found it. We then turned off the halogen lights and placed the fox-tethered key back in its drawer beneath the register. Aside from the toppled books in the back and the Valison novel that we had removed from its place on the shelf, Jorgen's shop harbored no signs of our intrusion. We locked the door before we closed it.

The snow still fell with an intensity similar to that which it had possessed prior to our entering the shop. Additionally, the wind had begun to blow a bit harder, imbuing the air with an increased chill. Mr. Wible lingered in the shelter of the doorway to light his pipe.

Across the street, we noticed a small fox slip out of the snow, down through a sewer grating that billowed steam. "I must review the Valison novel," Mr. Pacheco said, and Mr. Wible obligingly fished the plastic bag from his satchel before striking another match. After glancing again over the title for no more than a few seconds, Mr. Pacheco returned the book.

Mr. Wible finished puffing his pipe into life and deposited the spent matches in the pocket of his trench coat. "What is it?" he then enquired.

"The inscription on the title page," Mr. Pacheco responded, stifling a cough at Mr. Wible's smoke. "It may not be the volume's previous owner after all, but rather a concrete clue to the MacGuffin affair. Whatever the case, we must repair immediately to the Elite Café."

Mr. Wible harrumphed. Our Heroine's earlier presence in that establishment had determined it as the next item on our itinerary well before Mr. Pacheco's pronouncement.

BLAISE

It is this morning and I am sitting with Our Heroine at a table in the Elite Café. I have switched from coffee to tea. The bag leaks its reddish oils into the water of my glass. Our Heroine is murmuring platitudes about the death of my wife. Or perhaps she is not. It is difficult to listen to her.

"You've got a little..." She reaches across the table and dabs at my nose with her napkin, wet from the bottom of her teacup. I do not flinch. The napkin carries with it a spot of blue when she pulls it away.

"Thank you for saving me back there," she says. "I'm like a rabbit in the headlights with him. I just can't turn away even though I know he's going to run me over."

"You are welcome," I offer. She does not immediately respond.

Silence is an unusual state for her, despite her otherwise apparent reverence for words. She shifts uncomfortably in her seat, and I see that her hair is not quite dry. I do not think that it could have been so dampened by the snow. Ridiculously, I feel the sadness of how cold her ears must be and how cold my wife's ears must be also. Our Heroine sips her tea.

"You know, until yesterday, I felt like it was all over," she says. "That after my mother died there was no way this sort of thing could happen again. I felt like she had somehow been the one who drew bad things to us. It's been sixteen years."

She trembles slightly, and I think again of her hair; it is most often blond, but wetness has darkened it to brownish.

Shirley enjoyed cafés. Perhaps I desired the resemblance to normality that is demanded by a crowded room. I now wish I had chosen someplace other.

"Bad things have also happened in the past sixteen years," I say. "To all of us."

"I know." She looks up from her tea and into my eyes as she has looked into them once before. "But this is the worst thing."

There is nothing I can say. I am not on the verge of shouting, but her words resonate with my shouts of last night. I notice now the atmosphere of unreality that has surrounded me since first I heard that my wife was dead. Only the sound of my shouts can disperse it, and only for brief moments. It is the dullness of the pain. It is the worst thing.

"At least you know that she loved you," Our Heroine says, and the thing is abruptly worse. "She didn't just leave you behind of her own free will."

I gulp deeply of my tea and hold the liquid in my mouth until it has lost its heat. She is speaking only of the infidelity of Prescott. Unless—

"I'm sorry. I can't believe I just said that," she blurts. She is speaking only of the infidelity of Prescott.

I swallow. "It is copasetic," I say. "Prescott was not good for leaving you of his own free will."

YMIRSON

Emily. She was being held against her will by Surt. I had to save her. I remember this. As I emerged from the dark cavern my eyes were stung by the whiteness of the snow, and it was thus that I did not see the blackguard who had crept behind me even when I turned at the noise of him. There was no pain, but I was dizzy and I fell, and my face was clumsy from the snow. I still remember this.

When my eyes could see again at all, the light was blurred, but I saw Emily pulling rubber from the face of Surt. I saw something of his face. Then my daughter, turning me over and pulling me to my feet, spoke to me. The infernal reporter was there with her. "Let's just get him to your house," she said to my daughter, and then she said something to me.

"Are you all right, Mr. Ymirson?"

But I knew that she should not be spoken to, so I held my silence.

NATHAN

At first I just stood there in the Thing Room like an idiot, not saying anything, waiting for the father and son to finish chatting with their buddies. I figured they were probably discussing whether or not I'd get permission to see the real inner sanctum, and I didn't want to ruin my chances by saying anything stupid. But after a few minutes passed, and the son just got up and walked off down one of the side corridors without so much as a glance in my direction, I realized that I was gonna have to fend for myself for a while.

The room was like Grand Central with all the comings and goings; I felt pretty out of place the way everyone else was bustling around me. It was like the projector reel was being cranked back too fast and I was just about the only still thing in the frame. The woman and the old guy in the corner were pretty stable, too, I guess, and that's probably what drew my attention to them. But even the men in their little squatting groups kept getting up and shifting places, circling around each other... Splitting off and forming new circles. Everything just had this real restless quality to it. Frenetic. I had to walk across the room to shake the sensation.

The woman wasn't dressed like a native. This pissed me off a little, since I'd been so fervently assured that I was going to be the only outsider in here, but I decided not to make a big deal of it. I leaned up against the wall a few feet away from her and the old dude. He looked kind of familiar to me, but I figured it was probably just the way he reminded me of a generic old-school movie star. He had the traditional big-jawed good looks of a Kirk Douglas, or a Charlton Heston, or a Burt Lancaster. She seemed pretty engrossed in her conversation with him. I was so busy trying to figure out where I knew him from, though, that it took me over a minute to realize they were speaking English.

"But the second occurrence..." she said. Her voice was sort of shaky, like music from a sun-warped cassette. She might've been crying. "Well, I'm really not certain. I suppose—if I were to try to trace my own motivations in the matter—that I was attempting in some sense to demonstrate to myself—or, rather, to both of us—that the first occurrence hadn't in all actuality— Well, that I'd been in control. But I now apprehend the fact that I hadn't been. And that renders it all the worse, doesn't it? At least that's the way that all of the threads seem to resolve, to my mind. I'm not really great with interiority, though, so perhaps I'm reading it wrong. But I'm just rambling now. What's your opinion?"

"I have said before and I shall say again that it is not your fault. You cannot be held to blame for a dog's rabid turn. Hmph. You... I do not know what else to say. Dog and hound and cur. I must think for a moment." The guy's accent was surprisingly subtle considering that he must have been in his late thirties—at least—by the time Vanaheim was discovered. He was a quick learner, I supposed. Or else he was an Icelander, which would have explained his modern dress-style. I had trouble telling the accents apart.

"I've encountered you before, haven't I?" I noticed that her voice had lost its quaver. And then I noticed that she was addressing me. "Yes, yes; I know who you are. You're that *Hamlet* boy from Denmark."

I should have known I couldn't avoid my fans, I thought. Then I looked at her full in the face for the first time, and I realized that I actually did know her. She looked completely different outside of the library, though, with her hair down and her glasses removed. I really had met her in Denmark. She'd been researching *Hamlet*, too.

"Yeah," I said, pushing myself away from the wall. "Oh, hey. I didn't recognize you at first."

"Hmm... Your middle name wouldn't happen to be Michael or Elmo or Melvin, would it?" she asked me. Her eyes were a little red. The old guy seemed to have drifted off into his own little world.

"No," I said. "It's Green. Why do you ask?"

"Green? Hmm... Well, no, that simply won't do at all. I was attempting to contrive an apposite anagram for you, but I'm afraid you're short the "M" and the "L" needed for anything to do with *Hamlet*. But why don't you sit down and join us? Perhaps I can think of something while we talk. My companion and I were just discussing Vanatru theology."

CONSTANCE

With faux-Vanatru spirituality sweeping Hollywood, and everyone from Madonna to Cher overcoming fears of red-paint reprisals by boldly sporting designer fox-fur coats and accessories, and with even fitness guru Billy Blanks tossing aside Tae Bo in favor of Refurserkir-inspired "Fox Boxing," what could possibly be more chic than dating the daughter of the man who discovered the place? That's what Bean Day pilgrims were wondering this week when Hollywood heartthrob Nathan— no, I promised.

OUR HEROINE

I tried not to worry about my father, safely in Connie's care now, as I made my way downtown. Most of the Bean Day tourists were gone by the time I arrived; they'd already moved on to the more outskirtish sites, like the park where Prescott had almost married Gerd, or the burnt-down farm where Surt had buried his forged Viking weaponry. This meant that none of them were around to bother me for an autograph, but it also meant that none of them were around to tell me if they'd seen Garm. I'd decided to concentrate on Garm, while my other problems brewed in my brain. At least he was out here somewhere, running about—not being held captive by Refurserkir or some inept ring of antiquities thieves. All assuming I could believe Connie, of course.

Intellectually sexy. The snow still fell, but somewhere between here and home I'd stopped being angry about it. I supposed it sounded like something he might say. He'd learned most of his English from me.

"In Vanaheim, 'snow' is so all-around, it has many words," he told me once (I translate from the original Vanaheimic). "When its color cannot be seen and it moves as if with life in it, we call it *vatn*. When it is so cold that it is hard like stone, we call it *ís*. Only when it is soft and white do we call it *snjór*."

Intellectually cute.

Still, six months without a word, and I must admit I hadn't quite minded.

BLAISE

It is six months ago, and Prescott has returned to Vanaheim without saying goodbye to Our Heroine. She has come to me for comfort.

"I just don't understand," she says between heaves of sob. "I mean, I'm not dumb... I know that we weren't good together anymore. If we ever were, that is, and it wasn't just always us clinging to some dumb fantasy. And I know it just wasn't nearly as exciting since my... I know he had every reason to go. But why did he have to go? I just don't understand."

She has iterated her story many times. She does not understand; that alone is clear. The bottle of schnapps that she has brought with her is assuredly not contributing to her comprehension.

"Where's Shirley?" she asks. Her sobs have suddenly ceased.

"She is researching."

"Where? In her study? Out in the Two-Story House? Where?"

"She is out. I believe her intention was to visit your father at his library and then to retire to the Elite Café for a session of note-taking."

She looks into my eyes with a slight squint that suggests some amount of comprehension. Of what, I am uncertain.

"I'm sorry," she says, though I do not know why. Her eyes are streaked with the red of swollen veins and her mouth is half-open for breath. She has drunk too much.

"I do not understand," I reply.

NATHAN

"I don't get it," I said as I sat down Indian style, across from the woman and the old guy. "So, they worship dogs here or something?" She'd said they were discussing Vanatru theology, but it sure sounded to me like they'd been discussing hounds.

"Hmm? Well, there is a definite reverence for the Arctic fox," she said. "But no, it wouldn't be quite accurate to say that they worship them..." She paused, and then I think she realized why I'd asked—what I'd overheard her say before. "Their mythology does include quite a few stories with dogs and foxes in them, though... So, yes, I suppose I should have said that we were discussing Vanatru *myth*ology, rather than *the*ology. Pardon my lack of specificity."

"I am not fond of dogs," the old guy said.

The woman crawled down from her chair to sit with me across from him. "He's lying," she told me. "He's fairly fond of his own dogs, at least, but he likes to let on that he's too gruff and curmudgeonly for that sort of thing."

The guy snorted derisively, and she smiled up at him.

"So, enlighten our new acquaintance here with the wisdom that you were just about to impart upon me," she prompted. "About the Aesir and Vanir and all of that other crap."

"Hmph. Yes. I will tell you a story."

"Is there a dog in it?" I asked.

"When Christ came to Iceland," he started, ignoring my question, "Thor met him on the shore and challenged him to a fight, to determine which of them would rule.

"'I will not fight you,' Christ told Thor. 'If you strike me down now, I will only turn the other cheek.'

"'And that is why you will never conquer Iceland,' Thor replied, 'for I am the Hammer and you are the Nail.'

"But Christ was quick with reply and said to Thor, 'The Hammer was fine in Norway, where it was used to fell bears; what use is it, however, in felling a fish?'

"What Christ had seen and Thor had not seen was this:

with no other ready food in Iceland, the people would be able to survive only by the fish, and this was Christ. For he is both fish and fisherman. Even Thor could hear the wisdom in this, then, and he agreed to follow Christ. So this is why the two of them did not fight, and the country was built by both of them. Thor the Hammer and Christ the Nail."

"And Jesus was a carpenter, too," I added. The woman nudged me in the ribs with her elbow, though I'd been trying to sound interested rather than disrespectful. The guy's eyes had been dead before, unfocused, but they'd really lit up now that he was telling his story. Like De Niro when the camera's rolling.

"When Christ came to the Vanatru," he continued, "Frey greeted him hospitably.

"'Your people chew the bark of birches and sleep in clumsy dwellings,' said Christ. 'Join with me, and your people will enjoy the fruit of the sea, which is myself, and they will have a place in my father's house.'

"Frey thought on this, and he came near to agreeing, for it was true that his people desired something more than the meager crops that they were able to grow on the hard inland soil. At that moment, however, a fox happened by, and he began to bark at Christ and to tear at his robes. And when the robes came loose, Frey saw that Christ was truly Loki in disguise. Frey and the fox then chased him away, and he never returned to trouble the Vanatru. This was the same fox that taught the Vanatru to live beneath the ground and who taught them to eat of the ormolu lichen."

"But how did the fox know that Jesus was Loki?" I asked.

"His scent," the old guy answered. "Loki could change his

shape, but he could not change his scent. When he ran from the gods who sought to punish him, the final form he took was that of a fish.[31] That which the gods thought was Loki, and that which they chained beneath the earth, that was merely another fish that Loki had enchanted to seem as him. Loki was the fish that escaped, and afterward he changed his name to Christ."

SHIRLEY

I am a fish.

BLAISE

Bless your throat. The tale of St. Blaise and the fishbone. But what was the fishbone on which *I* was in danger of choking?

It is early this morning, and I have yet to depart for the Elite Café. I linger in my doorframe, pondering again what I at first took to be a simple salutation. *My aim is true.* There is something else beneath it, I am certain, but my thinking continually returns to other matters.

---

31. See also Jon Ymirson's translation of *Lokasenna*, "The Flyting of Loki." The story related above is mentioned in one of the extended footnotes as an example of the way in which myths and legends of mainstream Norse mythology have been appropriated and recontextualized by the Vanatru. *Lokasenna* itself tells the tale of how Loki insulted all of the other gods and was consequently punished by being tied to a stone beneath the earth where a serpent hung above his head dripping venom. His wife sat at his side with a bowl in which to catch the venom, but whenever the bowl became full and she was forced to turn away to empty it, the venom would sting his eyes, and his thrashings at the pain would cause earthquakes.

It is later this morning, and I have wasted too much time drinking tea. Our Heroine has suggested that she knows the name of Shirley's killer. She mentioned the name of Hubert Jorgen. I must find him. I do not believe that he was in Denmark or Iceland concurrently with Shirley, but I must find him nonetheless.

"Yeah," she has said to me. "But the thing is, even if I had a suspicion or an inkling, I couldn't tell you about it when you're like this, because you'd just go off and—"

"You have a suspect?"

"I— *know*. But my point is, what if I had a suspect and I was wrong? My dad's the same way, if he even had a vague idea about who did this, he'd just go and—"

"I must go now," I say to her. "I am sorry to depart with such brusqueness, but I have wasted too much time already. Thank you for consoling me, but catching the killer will be the thing that consoles me most."

"You're welcome, I guess..." She is obviously distraught, though it is in a way that I do not quite comprehend. Her eyes are open wide to me. "But you just got here... And I still wish you'd reconsider about doing this yourself."

I rise from my seat. I cannot reconsider. This is something that I must investigate for myself, for reasons apparent and otherwise. "I think I do know something of how you are miserable about Prescott," I tell her. "I am sincerely sorry that there is no killer to catch that would console you."

As I move toward the exit, the man with whom Our Heroine had been conversing upon my arrival raises his arm to wish me goodbye, but he lifts it only halfway before he stops to rub his shoulder. I believe his name is Boris Baxter.

He appears to be sick. Though the day is cold, still he sweats profusely.

WIBLE & PACHECO

The Elite Café bestowed upon us a pleasant sensation of warmth, which contrasted sharply with both the store of Hubert Jorgen—from which we had just come—and the continued snow of afternoon. Baxter had pushed four of the small café tables together to make room for his graduate student retinue. Discussion was well underway, having commenced around one o'clock according to our most reliable intelligence. A seemingly popular professor, there was little room for us to squeeze our way in, so we waited for caffeine to enact its diuretic effects on the weak-bladdered, and then quickly we assumed their seats.

"No, I'm sorry," Baxter said to a corn-haired coed, slapping the table and cutting her off mid-sentence. He dragged a napkin across his pale forehead as he spoke. We noticed that his thinning brown hair was in a state of severe disarray. "I'm afraid that just won't do. No more laudatory papers on Vanaheim qua Utopia, if you please. Vanaheim? Vana-ha! If you *must* write about the place, focus on something like the way it acts as a dark mirror to topside Iceland—a repressed yet physical subconscious—or the way that Iceland's obsession with purity is grotesquely manifested in Vanaheim's inbred royal family. That sort of thing. Anyway, that should be enough to get you started. Now, who's next?"

"If you would permit us," we ventured, "though not enrolled in any of your lectures, we would like to ask a few questions of you nonetheless."

"Yes, fine, but make it quick," Baxter answered, scrutinizing us with eyes asquint. "I'm not feeling very well, just now, and I'm afraid it's put me off my mood. I should probably be home in bed, except for the fact that my students depend on me so much. But please, ask away." Even through the narrow aperture of his squinted eyelids, we could see that his whites were extremely bloodshot.

His students looked to us with only perplexity upon their faces.

"You knew Shirley MacGuffin," we asserted.

He pressed his index and middle fingers hard against his temples and then emitted a series of noises, at this point, that we could only presume to be coughs, though in terms of objective description the sound was more akin to scraping metal.

"Ha. Ha, ha," he said flatly when he was finally able to speak again. We could not be certain whether he was laughing or clearing his throat. "I knew Shirley, it's true. But if you're trying to start an argument, I'm afraid you'll have to assert something a bit more controversial than that. For instance, did I kill her? No I did not!"

"You were assisting her in her attempt to emulate an apocryphal version of *Hamlet*," Mr. Pacheco stated, unshaken by Baxter's sudden shout.

"Ha. Ha, ha. You said you had questions for me; but I am still waiting to hear them. You haven't asked me any questions." He unsuccessfully attempted to transform his sickly expression into one of mild amusement, and he tensed the fingers of each hand one against the other, creating the shape of a coxcomb. Sigil of the Fool. We resolved to watch our step.

The students whose places we had taken now returned from the men's room and stood behind us. Mr. Pacheco restored to them their respective cappuccinos.

Affecting mild amusement ourselves, we continued our enquiry. "We are interested in this *Hamlet*. What can you tell us of it?"

"Hamlet? I like him not, nor stands it safe with us to let his madness range." He paused to spit a phlegmatic blob onto the table in front of himself. "But from the sound of things, you know more about the subject than I do. Shirley never showed me a single page."

"Yet she came to you for help regarding the project, did she not?"

"She came to me with *questions*." The tone of his voice was elevated to shrillness upon this final word, and he rolled his eyes wildly. "Specific questions, quite unlike the two of you. They mostly regarded subtle nuances of a dialect for which I have little love. Can we please stop talking around the subject, though? You want to know if I killed Shirley or if I have any information concerning her death. The answers are, respectively: *no!* And *no!* So will there be anything else, or does that just about settle it?"

His students collectively took in their breath, doubtless in anticipation of our response, which, as they sensed, could have been a scathing retort to his overly dramatic summation. We maintained a placid exterior, however, in order to provide greater counterpoint to his bombast.

"You misinterpret our intentions," we said. "Much though

we would welcome the killer being brought to justice, we are not ourselves engaged in the investigation of Ms. MacGuffin's murder. Rather, we merely seek certain documents that she was in possession of prior to her demise."

If this statement managed to disconcert him, the fact was not made apparent in his physiognomy. His expression had become progressively more pained throughout our interview, but it was with seemingly little relation to the actual words being said.

"For God's sake!" he exclaimed, banging the table with a weakly curled fist. "If it's *Hamlet* you're after, why don't you look to Denmark? What has Vanaheim got to do with anything? Leave me alone! Please!"

We made no answer; if this non sequitur was meant to perplex us, then it was successful. We decided to let him determine the manner in which the conversation would proceed.

"It was just a stupid idea," he mumbled, glancing down at the table and then spitting up a sort of black bile to join the greenish phlegm in front of him. The quiet of his comment provided a strange contrast to his previous outburst.

"Perhaps you are sicker than you realize," we offered. "But in any case, ideas in themselves possess no inherent level of intelligence. However, if you refer to Shirley's—"

Before we could complete our sentence, he snapped his face up and stared at us with widened eyes.

We had seen that exact sort of mortal fright once before.

"Kkkkkkkkkkkkkkk," he managed to say before his head fell finally back to the table.

We decided to leave before panic ensued in earnest and the police arrived on scene. Our concerns had never been with the physical or the mundane; we opted, therefore, to allow Baxter's students to deal with his body.

OUR HEROINE

I was just wandering aimlessly, now, with a semi-certain intuition that Garm had been killed by a snowplow. I could see it in my mind. He'd been chasing this other dog that Constance had seen, and it had lured him right beneath the wheels. I walked up Telegraph, keeping an eye out for any red discoloration in the snow.

It had let up a little. Falling constantly, but in smaller flakes, farther between. Still, it wasn't weather for anyone to be out in. Even a dog. Or a bastard like Hubert. I'd always thought bastard should mean "male dog." Bastard and bitch. At least I couldn't feel how cold my toes were.

The sun was just visible behind the sky, a dull quarter-slug above the red brick face of the Elite. I paused in the road to watch a kid replacing the letters on the cinema marquee. What attractions did the town hold that a dog couldn't find at home? Cats, perhaps. But where would cats be found out in this? The alleys, maybe, but the snow there was a bit too high for human slogging, so I discounted that idea without investigation. My eyes flicked down from the marquee to the cinema lobby and caught Wible and Pacheco about to emerge; I hurried down Dixon Lane, out of sight.

But wait. I went back and poked my head around the corner. Random wandering was getting me nowhere. If I was right about who hired them, then perhaps they actually had *some* clue about what they were doing. They were heading away from me, toward Vico. I waited until they turned (left) and then followed after. Perhaps they would stumble onto Garm or Hubert. Or something else worth finding. Too bad no crowds for me to hide in. I watched from a doorway until they turned up Masonic, and then I dashed after again. Exercise would do me good, anyway. And it was better than sitting at home and worrying.

CONSTANCE

All was well in Our Heroine's house. Jon Ymirson was snoring soundly in the spare bedroom, the wood-burning stove was successfully keeping away the snowy cold, and I—unable to quite get into the rhythm of typing up my notes—had decided to use this rare opportunity to take an innocent tour of the domestic atmosphere that had produced one of the most outstanding women of our time.

No.

Though Our Heroine's childhood adventures with her illustrious parents have been chronicled in some detail by Magnus Valison in the famous series of novels that he adapted from Emily Bean's true-life diaries, I am certainly not the first of her admirers to wonder about the more mundane events between adventures that helped shape her into the woman she was eventually to become. So, finding myself virtually alone in the house in which she grew up—the very model for her psychic architecture laid bare before me—how could I help but explore?

No. Too clunky. And not trite enough for my readership.

Though I have been acquainted with the Bean-Ymirson family for many years—my first encounter with them dating back to the early eighties when I was but a cub reporter, fresh out of high school and trying to make a name for myself by covering the spectacular homicide cases in which the family was prone to becoming embroiled—it wasn't until Emily Bean met her own bitter end in 1985 that I was truly treated as an intimate, joining with them in their time of mourning for this woman who meant so much to us all. Jon Ymirson, ever stoic, betrayed his affection for me only through his silent tolerance, but Our Heroine, closer to me in both age and temperament, welcomed me into the family with open arms. I came to feel much like an older sister to her in that time. And now I was in the house that I never got to grow up in, searching out the childhood that my sister and I never had the chance to share...

Bah! Screw it.

I began my snooping in the study.

BLAISE

It is well before the dawn of this morning, and study of my wife's journals has revealed me to be the cuckold.

I know the mind of my wife, and in her writings I can trace the manoeuvres with which she sought to hide her infidelity. I can sense the words that lurk beneath the layers of her ink that I cannot scratch away. Worse than both of these things, I can read plainly the passages where she did not seek to hide anything at all.

I can't tell Blaise about this, for instance. Or in the places where I must seek the beginnings of her words:

Feelings of rage, guilt... I'm very emotional. My eye feels oddly raw. What happened? All the horribly evil deeds I've done...

There is a feeling like anger and betrayal. It is like frustration. It is something interior, ineffable, and it yearns to be effed. I can only emit yells, instead.

His teeth were white as snow.

All my words shall be stallion, not a workhorse among them.

We must create incomprehensible things in order to have an analogy for our incomprehension of the universe. Obscure reality to make it more attractive. We must keep secrets, so that we may have the pleasure of uncovering them: wow.

K. It is more important that my work be marveled at than that it be understood.

Evil that we participate in freely in order to make ourselves believe that it is not evil after all.

More attractive. The workhorse and the stallion. The secret pleasure. The evil participated in freely. I have teased the meaning from each of these things.

Were she still alive I could forgive her.

The K presents difficulties of interpretation and appears often. The initial of a name would be too uncomplicated. Constant, for "Constance"? But Constance Lingus was not my wife's lothario.

His teeth were white as snow. As white as the snows of Iceland, perhaps. It occurred during the summer that she studied *Hamlet*. Shirley's words are clear in that regard. What other meaning could they hold? Less clear, however, is the identity of her lover. The identity of her murderer.

WIBLE & PACHECO

The mortal fright of Boris Baxter had recalled to our minds the first case on which we had cooperated with the Bean-Ymirsons: *The Case of the Consternated Cossacks*, as Magnus Valison had dubbed it in his literary adaptation of the events—the same adaptation that we had discovered in Hubert Jorgen's store. Having found this clue in the *store* of Hubert Jorgen, then, we decided to proceed onward toward his *house*—in order to see what other clues we might find among his possessions.

NATHAN

The old guy just kind of deflated when his story was done, let his eyes glaze over and fell back where he was sitting. It was like he'd been possessed while he was telling it, but now the demon had been exorcized. I didn't even realize who he was until way later, after I'd already caught my plane for the States and I found his face in the middle of some magazine stuffed into the back of the seat in front of me. And even then I could hardly believe that it had been him. At the moment, I just thought he seemed uncannily familiar. It kind of made me sad to look at him, like he could have been my dad or something. I shook it off, though.

"Well. How would you react if I were to suggest a walk?" the woman asked me, pushing herself halfway up on her hands.

"I'd probably say something like, 'Yeah, that'd be cool,'" I told her. My ass was getting numb anyway. I stood and took a glance around while she sat there, still resting on her hands.

I knew it probably wasn't the smartest thing to do, wandering off without my guides, but the son still hadn't returned, and I wasn't going to attempt to talk with the father on my own, especially since it looked like it was his turn to speak in the center of the little circle he was sitting in. I'd just have to try not to be gone too long.

"You have my immortal gratitude," the woman said to the old guy. "I'll be back later to discuss the matter with you further... If you're quite certain that you wouldn't mind."

"Yes, it is always nice to speak with you," he mumbled smiling up at her.

She grabbed her backpack from beneath the chair she'd been sitting in and pulled out a Maglite. "Ready?"

"Sure, where're we going?"

She gave me a funny look, then. Squinted with her whole face, like she'd just tasted a lemon or she was skeptical of something. But she didn't say anything; she just led me down the same corridor that the son had gone down. At least I thought it was the same corridor. It was pretty easy to get confused about direction down there.

We didn't say much to each other, at first. We just walked. She seemed to know where she was going, and her flashlight technique was a bit steadier than the father's had been, but she didn't seem to think there was anything worth chatting about along the way. The walls were still pretty barren, though, so I could kind of see her point. They were pretty narrow, too. I kept a few paces behind her.

"So... Keeping tabulations on me, are you?" she said after we'd gone a decent distance. She stopped and turned to face me. Her voice sounded serious all of a sudden, but with the light pointing at me I couldn't really make out her expression.

"What, you think I followed you here?"

"Yes. That is precisely what I'm suggesting. *Did* you follow me here? To Vanaheim, from Copenhagen?"

"I didn't even recognize you at first."

"So your answer to my question would be no, then?"

"Well, yeah my answer would be no. I mean, it is no. Why would I have followed you?"

She pointed the flashlight up beneath her chin before she spoke, like she was telling me a ghost story. "It just seems fairly... anomalous, is all. The two of us meeting in Denmark, and then you turning up here, only a few days after my own arrival... I suppose I'm just exhibiting signs of latent paranoia... Or is that just what you'd have me believe?"

I shuffled my shoes on the dirty floor. "Look, if you think I'm stalking you, well, don't worry. I'm used to it being the other way around, and I—"

"No. Wait. Fine." I saw her shake her head in silhouette. "Perhaps I should apologize; I wasn't suggesting that you were a stalker or that you were in any way the more psychologically impaired between the two of us, but it's just..." She turned the flashlight up at her face again and smiled. "Okay. I'm sorry. I'm acting all peculiar, amn't I? Come on. Just follow me."

She started back down the tunnel, and I trotted after her. I figured it was best not to say anything at all. It was getting more humid, but I couldn't smell sulphur anymore. My nose must have been getting used to it.

OUR HEROINE

I hadn't tailed anybody in a long time, and I wasn't really used to it anymore. It was a wonder that they didn't make me. Pacheco was walking in the lead, about a block and a half ahead, and every time he looked over his shoulder to say something to Wible I did my best to duck behind the nearest telephone pole or postal drop-box, but I was probably drawing more attention to myself than if I'd just walked nonchalantly. At least the action kept me warm.

I got so wrapped up in trying to conceal myself without looking ridiculous to the occasional passerby, though, that I hardly noticed we were moving out of the downtown area until the drop-boxes became so scarce that I had to start ducking behind snowdrifts. We were headed back in the direction from which I'd come. Were they on their way to visit me? Maybe I should just jump out and let them see me to save us the walk. But then they turned up Lanark Road, which didn't lead anywhere near my house. Odd.

WIBLE & PACHECO

Though in this world there are phenomena that might justly be termed "strange," there are no phenomena that cannot—given sufficient information—be explained. This is not to suggest that for every effect there is a cause, of course. That is an assumption that we are not prepared to make, lest it launch us ineluctably down the path of determinism. This is only to suggest, rather, that there is no "thing" that exists without some relation to at least one other "thing," and it is the matrix of a "thing's" relationships that determines its meaning in the larger context of the world. Even something strange can be explained by tracing its relational lines of flight, however casual or causal they may be.

Thus, while we found it strange that we were being followed by one of the subjects of our investigation, we assumed that—as more information came forth—an explanation would manifest itself, and we saw no cause to effect any immediate change in our course of action. It did cause us to wonder, however, what this subject's relationship was—if any—to the librarian, Hubert Jorgen, whose store had proven so fruitful and to whose house we still were heading.

BLAISE

It is early in the spring of 1998, and I am assisting in the erection of the Two-Story House.

The foreman is discussing the blueprints with Shirley. She is worried that the completed structure will not adequately serve her purpose. I sense that the workers are annoyed by her, though she has brought out pitchers of fresh lemonade. Perhaps it is bitter. No one has tasted it, as of yet. The foreman is explaining again why her original plans were impracticable. On the upper level, Jon Ymirson—bare-chested in the unseasonal humidity of late March—swings a hammer, driving nails into wood, affixing one plank to another. Jack stud, king stud. He is constructing the frame of what will become a doorway. He is more competent than me in the building arts, and the workers have taken to him as one of their own. Shirley frowns at the exasperated foreman.

At least the workers are not lusting after her. She is quite attractive in her baggy white T-shirt and paint-spattered work jeans. Unless they can lust through their annoyance.

My fingers are numb from the vibrations of the electric saw with which I have been trimming boards for the last twenty minutes. My eyes are sweat-filled and my goggles fogged.

Sawdust clings to my hands, and its smell to the hairs of my nose. I decide to rest a moment. Though the other workers labor on, I set aside my saw and walk to the picnic table upon which my wife has laid the refreshments.

In addition to the lemonade, she has supplied a box of donuts. Of these, the workers have deigned to partake.

I remove a plastic cup from the red tower between the pitchers and fill it with lemonade. Most of the ice has melted already. I lick the salt from my moustache before taking my first sip. My wife glances up at me and meets my eyes across the cup's upper rim. The lemonade is sweet, and I drain the cup before it leaves my lips.

My wife smiles as I dip the ladle for a second serving. The smile contains gratitude, and shame, and love. It spans the distance between her thoughts and her actions. Her eyes turn back to the blueprints, but the smile lingers in the corners of her mouth.

I comprehend the ways in which Shirley can be an annoyance to others. I know how she allows herself to be perceived by them. But it is my pleasure that no others—not even Emily Bean-Ymirson in her lifetime—have understood the ways in which Shirley could never be a true annoyance to me.

CONSTANCE

Our Heroine has always been a bit secretive, but for many that's a huge part of her allure; something in that rare smile of hers conveys the sense that she knows a lot more than she's letting on, and that if you're lucky she just might give you a hint as to what it is. I didn't have much idea of what she wasn't letting on about this time—and she was still out searching for her dog, so no hint was likely to be forthcoming—but I assumed it to be identical with whatever it was that I was frustratedly looking for.

That is to say, I didn't know exactly what I was looking for, but it was quite frustrating not being able to find anything worth the searching. One expects the homes of celebrities to burble over with scandal buried clumsily just beneath the surface, but, sadly, this isn't always the case. Regardless, I kept on digging.

I felt that whatever I was looking for must have had something to do with the misfortune of Shirley MacGuffin, else Our Heroine wouldn't have been so adamant earlier about not discussing it. "But what angle could she have on the matter?" I wondered. Perhaps she was attempting to find Shirley's murderer, though it did seem a bit unlikely that she would willingly take on any task that could so easily be labeled an "investigation." Still, it was a definite possibility, and I was determined to resolve whether or not it was an actuality. There may have been many things that I did not know, but I was fairly certain of one thing: Our Heroine was searching for something more than just her dog. And that something had to do with the investigation of Shirley's murder. Maybe.

I sat down on the vinyl-upholstered couch across from the fireplace and glanced around the room for anything that I might have missed upon my initial pass. I hadn't known how much time I would have when I'd begun my snooping, so I'd limited myself to the simple things, wasting no effort on the likes of locked drawers in the desk or looking for hidden catches on the apothecary table. There had, after all, seemingly been enough out in the open to rummage through; the only problem was that, on closer examination, everything in the open had turned out to be rather innocuous.

A box of letters lay invitingly open on the mantel next to an ugly rusted candelabrum, but all that it had contained was correspondence from ex-students and colleagues at other universities. A pad of paper sat on the desk—with a good rubbing pencil handy beside it—but a careful glance-over revealed no indentations worth trying to bring out in relief. Apparently Our Heroine knew enough to remove pages from the pad before recording her thoughts.

Yet there had to be something in this room that I wasn't supposed to see. Surely it was just a matter of looking in the right place. "Perhaps I should try to open the desk after all," I thought.

As I started to push myself up off the couch, however, my hand felt something hard between the cushions. Glancing down at the crack, I saw Our Heroine's planner wedged within. Well, here was *something*. Settling back down onto the cushion, then, I opened the little booklet up, keen to see what secrets lay hidden between its ebon plastic covers. Oh, dear.

The empty, unplanned days ahead suggested that her social life was far less active than her recent spate of men had led me to believe. The only engagements slated beyond the date of Shirley's death were some doctor's appointments for her dad and a meeting with Blaise Duplain that had occurred this morning at the Elite Café; otherwise it seemed that her next few months were completely free. I flipped back a few pages to see if her past was as depressing as her future.

She'd taken a day-trip into the City about a week and a half ago, though she hadn't recorded her specific motivation.

Probably just clothes shopping. A few days after that, however, she'd had dinner with Shirley MacGuffin. This added some weight to my assumptions that she was somehow involving herself in investigation of the murder. Their appointment had most likely been some sort of girls' night out, I imagined, though I hadn't been invited. Probably one of their exclusive little "literary critiquing" sessions. But even more compelling than these appointments themselves was the "Notes" section that faced the planner's calendrical portion. Across from her dinner date, Our Heroine had jotted down some thoughts, and one paragraph in particular caught my eye:

"Our mutual 'literary critique' is going better than I expected, though Shirley's upset that someone apparently 'broke into her house' and stole one of her early drafts. It was just a word-for-word translation, though, so it's not like she can't just go look it up in a library. About my thing, though, Shirley thinks that the bit about the rusty 'candelabra (cadabra)' is a bit heavy-handed. Coming from her... She suggests that if I'm going to keep the passage at all, I should at least tuck it away in some hidden corner of the text where the reader will have to search it out. Make it a 'secret passage.'"

I placed the planner back between the cushions whence I had plucked it. "Secret passage, eh?" I couldn't help but mumble to myself. I stood up and walked back over to the mantel. The candelabrum atop it was rather rusty. Surely it couldn't be so simple.

NATHAN

The exterior of the temple had been so ornate, I kept expecting something similar from the interior, even after the disappointment of the Thing Room; I guess that's why the stark beauty of the steam pool caught me so off guard, just glowing there in the darkness with patches of ormolu in and all around it.

"So," she said, switching off the flashlight. "In relation to all else you've seen in Vanaheim, how would you appraise this particular locale?"

"I thought ormolu lichen didn't grow in here," I said.

"You do realize that Vanaheim is the only place on Earth where ormolu lichen *does* grow, don't you?"

"Yeah, but I don't know; it's just something my guide told me. That the Temple of the Refurserkir was cursed to eternal darkness by the troll who built it, and that that's the reason no lichen grows in here. Except now you show me this room, and it turns out that lichen does grow in here."

"I see. And you believe in trolls?"

"Well, no, but—"

"Shall we immerse ourselves, then?"

"Is that allowed? I mean, don't you think this is probably a sacred pool or something?"

"In all likelihood. Which might explain why the lichen grows in here, if your story has any element of truth to it... I suppose we'd have to ask someone, were we to desire surety on the matter. But I'm of the opinion that we should just let the Refurserkir have their secrets about such things. Some questions are better left unanswered."

"Um, okay," I replied. "But don't you think it's probably too sacred to swim in, then? Or, I mean, as long as we're not sure, shouldn't we err on the side of sacredness?"

She turned up one corner of her mouth in this little half

smile. "Well, the fact remains that the Refurserkir have let me use this pool in the past. Based on this precedent, I don't imagine that they'll be overly upset if they find me using it again, Q.E.D. Thus, I, at least, am going in."

She unbuckled her belt[32] and whipped it free of her pant-loops in one quick motion.

I felt kind of dumbfounded, and that was a weird feeling for me, because I pretty much always know what to say. "I don't have a bathing suit," I told her. She was hopping on one foot now to remove the shoe from the other foot.

"Well, I presume that you're at least wearing some manner of underclothing. Aren't you?"

"Yeah, but... I just don't understand what this is all about. I mean, I thought a walk would... Well, you know, my guides are probably wondering where I am, and—"

"Bathing is a hallowed act among the Vanatru. Frey's father was the god of baths or something. Don't you want to make sure you get the complete Vanaheimic experience?"

She undid the bottom button of her shirt and started working her way upward.

"No, it's just... I mean, I hardly know you, and—"

She stopped with two buttons left to go. "I'm not on the verge of seducing you, if that's what you're trying to imply. I'm simply suggesting that you and I should relax in a steam pool together. And, perhaps—while immersing ourselves—we can converse a bit."

"I see..." I just stood there for a second, trying to think of the right way to put it. I didn't want to offend her. "Um...

---

32. !!

I still think that sounds, perhaps, a bit too intimate."

"Look," she said. Stern face now. No more messing around, I took it. "Get this straight. Allow me to phrase it in plain language. I'm not trying to be 'intimate' with you at all, okay? I'm married." She held up her left hand to display a ring of white gold. "I do not aim to cheat on my husband. I love him, and I have never had any intention of betraying him. I do not wish to have sex with you, I don't wish to kiss you, nor do I so much as wish to hold your hand. I simply wish you to get into the steam pool with me and sit there for a while."

I looked at her for a second and didn't say anything at all. Then I sat down on the ground and unlaced my boots.

"All right," I said. "I guess it's not really that big a deal."

WIBLE & PACHECO

The house of Hubert Jorgen, as opposed to his shop, was rather large. We did not know the range of income typical of a person in the profession of dealing in rare and antiquarian books, but our intuition told us that it was substantially lower than that which would afford one a home of this size, design, and location. It was possible, of course, that the net monetary influx of his shop was not Jorgen's sole source of capital, though we were unaware of any other.

Despite our assumptions that no one would be inside the house and that we would only be able to enter via some indirect route (e.g., a window), we ascended the stoop and knocked on the front door; a full minute of inaction then followed, during which we received no response. We next tried the doorknob but discovered it to be locked.

Our initial assumptions thus confirmed, we were left with no recourse but to confront Our Heroine, who was hiding behind a telephone pole half a block away and who would need to be distracted before we could make any additional attempts at illicit entry. We went back down the walk and headed in her direction.

"Good lord!" Mr. Wible exclaimed—perhaps too exuberantly—once we came so close to the pole that feigning further ignorance of her presence lost its plausibility. He allowed his pipe to drop from his mouth as he spoke and then fumbled on the ground after it.

"Please pardon my partner's exclamation," Mr. Pacheco said. "We were unaware, however, that we were being followed."

OUR HEROINE

"Followed?" I asked. "I wasn't following you."

Wible pulled a tin of tobacco from an inner coat pocket and refilled his pipe.

"Of course not. Were you on your way to visit the librarian, Hubert Jorgen, then? We have just come from his door, ourselves, and were disappointed to learn that he is not at home."

"He's not really a librarian these days, you know.[33] But I was just out taking a walk. I'm looking for my dog. You haven't seen any strays about, have you?"

Wible tried to strike a match with his thumb, but it wouldn't spark, so he just ended up using the side of the matchbox. It took him two matches before he got a good coal burning.

"Hmm. We did notice a fox earlier, running astray in the

33. She needn't belabor the point.

downtown area, but your infamous dachshund did not appear to be anywhere in the vicinity."

"Well, I'd appreciate it if you'd keep an eye out for him while you're wandering around."

"You have our word. If we find your dachshund, we shall return him to you at once."

"So, what did you guys want to see Hubert about?"

"It was our wish to question him regarding the same matter of which we spoke with you earlier; we believe he may possess some degree of knowledge on the subject."

"About the mysterious documents, right?" As I said this, I realized that I'd allowed myself to become so caught up in the intrigue of following them, that I had allowed my mind to wander from the *tragedy* of Shirley's death. Which was precisely what I'd hoped to avoid. Wave of guilt and sadness washed simultaneously over me.

"We do not assume that you have reconsidered our proposal to relieve you of the danger and responsibility that accompany the custodianship of those documents?" Wible asked.

"Well, I'm admittedly a little curious about the fact that your investigation appears to involve Shirley, me, *and* Hubert, but—as I still have no idea what these documents are that you're searching for—you're safe in assuming that I haven't reconsidered handing them over to you."

"Of course. Since you insist on maintaining this charade, perhaps we should allow you to return to your search while we proceed with our own."

"Actually, you know, I'm kind of stumped as far as my search goes. Garm didn't exactly leave any clues regarding where he was headed. But how are you guys doing? You haven't seen already Hubert today, have you? Or are you just trying to contact everyone who might possibly be involved with... whatever?"

"Why do you ask? Are you aware of his whereabouts?"

"No, I'm just curious... I mean, aside from the fundamental flaw of your assumption that I have the documents, how is the search coming along?"

"It goes as it will. We gather points of information and trust that eventually we will be able to draw the proper connective lines between them; once we observe the full figure that these lines trace, our goal will have been met."

"Aha. That's nice. Keep it abstract and you don't need to worry about tangible results."

"You misunderstand. We—"

"No, it's okay. I get it. Mystery metaphysicians and all that."

"That is not a term we would apply to ourselves."

"I'm sorry. No offense was meant."

"You needn't concern yourself with the intricacies of our methods. If you decide that you wish to assist us in the full degree to which you are capable—namely by providing us with the documents for which we search—then shall we reveal to you the full scope of our knowledge, including the particulars of how you, Hubert Jorgen, and Shirley MacGuffin all fit into the picture that the lines of our knowledge trace. Until that time, however, we must keep certain details hidden to all but ourselves."

"Hmph. And your employer, right? You did mention earlier that someone hired you."

"If you mean to cast aspersions upon the purity of our

motives, please be assured... Though it is true that this investigation was begun at the behest of another, it is for our own reasons that we pursue it now. Our employer has become... incidental to the case, and you need not refrain from cooperating with us on that basis. Our intentions are—as ever—noble."

"You still ultimately answer to her, though, don't you?"

They paused before answering. "We are not deceived by your use of such a definite pronoun; you do not know the identity of the one who hired us."

"I—"

"..."

"Never mind. You're right; I don't know who she is. And it's none of my business, either. I should just stick to looking for Garm. Sorry to have bothered you guys." I turned to walk away.

"It is a positive sign, at least, that you show more curiosity regarding the matter than you did this morning," Pacheco called after me. "Perhaps, as your interest grows, you will come to see that cooperation with us is the wisest option available to you. For the time being, however, my partner and I wish you success in locating your dog."

When I turned around, they were already walking the other way.

BLAISE

It is late this afternoon, and I am lumbering through the snow of my backyard, approaching the Two-Story House. I am confident that Shirley's clue of "fish" will lead me to the answer not only of what happened in Denmark but also to the identity of her murderer.

Bless my throat. *I am a fish*, amid the Danish notes. And the two stories of the house each were concerned with fish.

The front door of the structure has no lock, but it is swollen with moisture and does not open when I turn the knob. Anger has begun to thaw the dullness of my pain. I shove against the door, and the thin wood shudders before swinging inward.

I have come here because it was begun immediately before Shirley departed to Denmark two and half years ago and it was completed immediately upon her return. I hope that here I may unearth the seeds of her betrayal. I have come here to find the fish on whose bone I choke.

I enter the house along with snow, and the floor is already wet from where previous snow has melted. Likely the door's bottom edge is too far from the floor, an unsealed aperture. The house was not designed for living.

Heat, among other amenities, is noticeably absent, and I have bundled myself in preparation. My hands are encumbered in snow gloves made even more awkward by my bandage, and I wear woolen socks within my boots. Additionally, a scarf which is the only thing that Shirley ever knit for me itches my unshaven neck. Despite all of this, I am cold.

I am beginning to realize the full import of things. Of all the desires that will never be met. I want to have Shirley now, and entirely. I want to know the things that she thought yet never said, and every urge that once occurred to her. I want to hear the story that she wrote alone in the sands of low tide while we were on our honeymoon and I slept late after a night of much exertion. I want to know of all the times when she watched me sleep and thought how easy it would be to smother me if she were evil. I realize that she will never be here to tell me of these things and that she will never be here for me to forgive her for what I have come to suspect she did.

The Two-Story House is so called because it is meant to tell two stories, and also because it is built of two floors. Shirley explained the premises to me often as we ate our breakfasts, though I have never explored them thoroughly.

I press the door to a close behind me and walk across the living room. The silence of the house is outlined by my boots upon the wooden floor. I have seen the interior before, but I have never paid close attention to its details. All objects with which the house is furnished are overlaid with words—sentences printed neatly upon them in inks of various color. There are four varieties in total: yellow, blue, green, and red. I do not know what significance is carried in the color of a given sentence, but yellow is by far the most prevalent.

For example, in the dining room, there is a small table with two chairs. Upon one chair is written such things as "(Yellow) She sat down across from him," "(Green) She shifted uncomfortably in her seat," "(Red) She pushed her chair from the table." On the other, "(Yellow) He sat down," "(Green) He curled his legs beneath his seat," "(Yellow) He picked up his plate and got up from his chair." The table itself reads, "(Yellow) Dinner tonight consisted of salmon, asparagus, and fried mushrooms," "(Yellow) He helped himself to another piece of fish; he hadn't even asked for the first but had rather just assumed that it was his by right," "(Red) She crumpled up her napkin and threw it down on the table," "(Blue) Her fork dropped from her hand," "(Green) He slid the cup of asparagus sauce across the table's surface," "(Blue) He set his glass directly down, forgetting the coaster beside his plate," "(Red) He swirled his asparagus tip violently around the bottom of the sauce-cup." The handwriting is small and neat.

Shirley originally planned to include yet greater detail, to fill the house with such props as the plates and serving platters and other utensils with which her characters had supposedly eaten. In the interest of frugality, I convinced her that an uncluttered home would evoke a greater sense of mystery.

I move from the dining room back to the living room and sit down upon the couch; pieces of the stories are stitched into the fabric that covers the cushions. Rising dust tickles my nose, but I cannot sneeze. By focusing on each sentence, I am able to ignore that which brings me to read them. "(Blue) He dug beneath the cushions for the remote but came up empty." "(Green) He sat down next to her and laid his head in her arms." I quickly see that no action of any relevance to me is described here, and neither is there any word of any fish on whose bone I might choke. So I rise and walk to the kitchen.

The two stories of the house are built one on top of the other, each involving the same two characters who are never named, taking place on consecutive days. The first story, chronologically, is—I believe—a mundane tale of domestic life that culminates in a moment of psychological revelation. The second is some sort of murder mystery in which even the identity of the victim is unclear. These facts I know from reading Shirley's journals, as well as from vague recollections of her breakfast babble. The interrelatedness of the two stories makes it difficult to discern where one ends and the other begins. Indeed—other than its name—the house contains hardly any clue that the stories are separate at all.

For instance, written upon the kitchen countertop, I see "(Blue) She sponged up the blood." Taken alone, this would seem to be a piece of the mystery, the hiding of evidence. Other sentences in its vicinity, however, suggest that the blood is merely from the woman's thumb, which she accidentally cut while slicing mushrooms for dinner. Further complicating matters, no indication is given of which story this mushroom dinner takes place in; it is possible, even, that the couple ate mushrooms on both nights. I am confident that such little ambiguities would remain even were I to read every sentence in the house.

But I am not here to merely enjoy the stories of my wife. I have indicated already why I am here, and I must hold true to my aim. Yet even in the kitchen, where the fish was cooked and prepared, that which I search for is not to be found.

I realize that I am tired, but I cannot rest. Perhaps I should drink more coffee. Or tea. I decide to explore the upper floor.

CONSTANCE

With a turn of the rusty candelabrum, a wooden panel beside the fireplace slid soundlessly open, revealing the foot of a spiral staircase within that wound upward into darkness. Could I risk stepping inside, not knowing if I'd be ever be able to get out again should the door somehow slide shut behind me? I could and would, but not without a light. Plucking a half-melted candle from the mantelpiece, I ran to the kitchen to rummage for a match.

Jon Ymirson was already there.

"Oh, hello," he said.

"Mr. Ymirson, how are you?"

"I am looking for something... Have you seen my belt?"[34]

"No, I'm afraid I haven't. Why don't you go lie in bed, though? I'll look around and bring it to you when I find it."

"Hmph. But it is imperative that I find it immediately. Or something else with which to— I cannot go out like this in such weather." At least he was lucid enough to realize that flannel long johns wouldn't keep him warm in the snow.

"But I don't think you should be going out at all," I told him. "It's quite cold. Besides, you've had a long day, and you need to get some rest."

"That is impossible. I cannot rest until I have found him."

"Well, your daughter is out looking for him as we speak, and despite what she may think of herself, she's actually quite a capable woman; you've no need to worry."

"How is that? But my daughter should not be involved in this at all! I must find her as well, then."

At precisely this point, the doorbell rang.

"Just one moment, Mr. Ymirson. Let me go get that, and I'll be right back to discuss this with you."

"But there is no need for further discussion," he murmured sadly to himself as I wandered from the room.

I didn't recognize the old man on the door's other side, but he introduced himself as Dr. Lorenz, a colleague of Our Heroine's, and he inquired whether she was home.

"No, she's not in right now," I told him. He just stood there in the snow, wiping his red bulbous nose with a flowery handkerchief, hugging himself to stop his shivering. He

---

34. !!!

looked a bit pathetic, really, and in my kindheartedness I couldn't help but invite him in. "She should be back shortly. So I suppose you could come in and wait," I said.

"That's very kind of you to offer," he replied, stepping spryly into the mudroom. "And I think I'll take you up on it." He knelt down to remove his shoes.

"Are you acquainted with her father?" I asked.

"I know of him, of course, though we've never met. Is he here?"

"Yes... Shall I introduce you to him, then?"

"Oh, please do."

So I led him bobbling into the kitchen to meet Jon Ymirson, still standing there, rubbing his hands and biting his lower lip.

"Dr. Ymirson, I'd like you to meet Dr. Lorenz."

"Hmm. It is nice to meet you."

"And it's very nice to meet you, Dr. Ymirson. I've followed your career with great avidity."

"Oh. That is nice."

"Why don't you gentlemen take a seat?" I motioned across the counter in an expansive gesture toward the living room. "I'll put some water on for tea. I just have a bit of business to finish up in the study, and then I'll be right out to join you."

"That would be lovely. What do you say, Dr. Ymirson?"

"Okay."

"Great," I declared. I then led Jon Ymirson to a chair, and Dr. Lorenz followed, proceeding to take a seat on the couch. I myself returned then to the kitchen and filled Our Heroine's well-worn kettle with water. I must note, here, that I filled it all the way to the top, precisely in order to give myself the maximum amount of time before it boiled, and I only turned the stove flame to medium with the same purpose in mind. It was then that I noticed a box of matches sitting on a shelf above.

"When do you expect Our Heroine to arrive?" Dr. Lorenz asked as I pocketed the matchbox.

"I'm not sure exactly," I replied, "but I imagine she'll be home in the next half an hour or so."

"Ah, excellent."

"Now, I'll be right back," I told them, and I headed down the hall.

"So, you discovered Vanaheim..." I heard Dr. Lorenz say as I closed the study door behind myself. Without a moment's hesitation, then, I proceeded to the passage, up the spiral staircase, finally toward whatever secret Our Heroine had to hide.

NATHAN

"So..." I said, trying to hide just how uncomfortable I was sitting in a steampool with this woman I didn't know.

"Thus," the woman replied. Her voice was quiet, like she was content to just sit there in silence, but she looked me in the eyes when she spoke. Inquiringly.

I glanced around us at the lichen growing on the walls and beneath the water. It was sparser and dimmer than the stuff that had covered the ceiling outside the Temple, and I wondered if it might be some other species that just imitated the ormolu.

Her bra and panties were black. I figured this meant that they wouldn't be too transparent—and there wasn't much light to shine through anything, anyway—but I was trying not to look. She was still looking at me, though, pupils wide, when I turned my eyes back toward hers.

"This feels pretty good," I said, finally. "I hadn't realized just how cold I was."

She didn't answer but just leaned back in the natural seat formed by the rocks around her and closed her eyes. I tried closing mine, too, but the heat just made me feel dizzy, so I immediately opened them up again.

"Whoa." I yawned then, but I wasn't feeling tired. It just felt good to breathe deeply. So I yawned again. I realized I probably wasn't getting enough oxygen, keeping my gut sucked in.

The air was heavy with steam, too, and I let my head nod. Rolled it around on my neck, trying to loosen up. It was hard to make out the shape of the cave around me as my eyes moved over it; it was hard to tell how far away the walls were. When I looked back down at my belly, though, I noticed that the green glow from the lichen was playing on my skin from all different angles, and it made these weird patterns as it refracted through the water... Reverse shadow puppets, and I could kind of control them by tapping my fingers on the steam-pool's surface like it was a typewriter. I started in home row and tried spelling out some words. "Reyklaug." "Spectral." "Kaleidoscopic."

"Is there supposed to be some buried meaning in that pattern of words?" the woman asked. "Because I'm afraid I fail to find any surface meaning in it whatsoever."

I looked up at her. She was staring me in the eyes again, and I realized that I must have been speaking the words aloud.

"No. I was just babbling," I said. "Why do you ask?"

She was scrutinizing me pretty closely, I realized.

"Are you feeling completely well?" she asked.

"Hmm. Yeah, you know. Just dandy. I guess I am feeling a little light-headed, though, now that you mention it. But is that necessarily a bad thing?" I laughed.

I noticed suddenly that I could make out the shapes around me a lot more clearly than I'd been able to only a few moments before. Apparently my eyes were adjusting.

"So, are you quite positive that you didn't follow me here from Denmark?" she asked, distracting me.

"What? No, I already told you that. Why would I follow you?"

"For what purpose, then, *did* you come here?" Her pupils were really large and black, and she was sitting up again, leaning toward me... Almost hovering above me, even. I might have cowered a little.

"Um... I just wanted to visit, I guess." I took a deep breath and blew it out. I was feeling really alert all of a sudden. I could feel the steam loosening up the phlegm in my lungs, and I breathed forcefully in and out a few more times. "Man, I don't even want a cigarette," I said, and I coughed emphatically.

"Well, that's fortuitous, I suppose, as I don't have any to offer. Yet you still haven't really answered my question, have you? What impetus set you upon your path? Why did you come here? Concentrate, now."

"Geez, I don't know... No, wait. I do. Part of the reason that I wanted to come here, I guess, was that—while I was in Denmark—I started reading a lot of Magnus Valison novels. And he talks about this place quite a bit. No. He writes about this place quite a bit. I don't know what he talks about. I've never even talked to him."

"Hmm... Well, you should give it a try; he's a skilled conversationalist. I can't truthfully say that I care much for any of his novels—at least not since *Dora, or Dara*[35]—but he is an entertaining person with whom to speak."

"You don't dig the *Memoirs*? Why not? I thought they were great. Like Tony the Tiger. Grrreat!"

"That's irrelevant to the conversation at hand. Besides which, I don't believe it would be very fruitful for us to argue tastes..."

"Mmm. I like that. The taste of fruit. Peaches."

She gave me a funny look. "So that's really the only reason you came here, then? Because you read some Valison novels?"

"Yeah, I swear. I thought they were amazing. All deep and shit. So why don't you like them? I don't want to argue tastes, I just really want to know. Because you're crazy for not liking them. Or maybe dumb. But, no, you don't *seem* dumb."

"Well, fine. If you really need some way to rationalize opinions that you find unfathomable, I'll give you one; Emily Bean was a staunch feminist."

I didn't follow, and the look on my face must have conveyed this.

She sighed before continuing. "So. Based on this fact, I don't believe that she would have been very pleased with the utterly masculine structure of Magnus Valison's novels. At least the ones that he wrote about her. They're all built around the traditional Western narrative paradigm of the male sexual experience... The slow build up to an orgasmic climax... I sus-

35. *Dora, or Dara: A Family Romance*, published in 1970, was one of the Master's greatest novels prior to the *Memoirs*.

pect Emily would have preferred him to render her story in a more concave, feminine manner."

"Okay, but what would that be? I mean, how is the female sexual experience so different from the male one?"

"Well, I presume that you *have* had sex?"

"Well, sure, yeah... And, I mean, I know it's *different* but... Well, please go on. I have nothing productive to add."

"Well, in order to put it in concrete terms, let me describe to you the choices that I would have made, had I been the one to adapt her diaries."

"Shoot."

"Okay, first of all, I would have shaped the stories such that they culminated climactically, but I would not have allowed that climax to be the sole focus of the book. I'd concentrate more on the full process of the act of love—figuratively speaking, of course—and less on the orgasm itself. With less of an ejaculatory, post-coital let down, as well... Ideally, then, I would leave the reader turned on with a few unresolved strands that might lead to further climax upon intense reflection of the experience. More negative space. What is not said placed on a level of equal importance with what is said. The suggestive... And perhaps some form of narrative cuddling afterward."

"Huh. Interesting... But, oh yeah. The other reason is that I got into a fight."

"Pardon?"

"I'm sorry. But you were asking me earlier about why I came here. And that's the other reason. I read some Magnus Valison novels, and I got into a fight. An argument, actually. But I was totally right, and she was totally wrong."

"I see." It came out sounding like a sigh.

"I was stupid, and I just took off without settling things with the person I fought with, though. So I should probably go back, you know? I think she's still there. But, yeah, that's part of why I came here. I'm sorry, though. You were saying something... Why did *you* come here?" I stretched my arms out and accidentally let my stomach expand, but I quickly sucked it back in. It felt really good to stretch, though, and I yawned again.

"Why did I come here? Well..." She turned her eyes downward and let out a little harrumph. "I just needed to get away from Denmark. I have friends here that I wanted to talk to."

"Cool," I said. "You know what, though? I'm feeling great. Doesn't this make you feel great? I mean, just sitting here. I feel so... nope, I can't even put it into words. Grrreat!"

"Well, you're basically soaking in ormolu tea.[36] It's a neural stimulant of some sort; I don't know the details of how it works... But it can be a bit overwhelming at first."

"Huh. That's really weird. But is it your job to sell this stuff or something? I mean, was this part of your sales pitch, getting me to come soak in this with you? Because if it is, I'm

---

36. A potent and pungent tea (gaining popularity in topside Iceland, though it has yet to make a successful market-shift to the United States) can be made by boiling dried bits of ormolu lichen. Hubert Jorgen, during his extended stay among the Vanatru, was the first to chronicle this and the many other applications to which the remarkable lichen is put in Vanaheimic society: not excluding, of course, the details of its use in a multitude of tasty meals. Indeed, as nearly no other natural food-source is to be found anywhere in the vicinity of Vanaheim (save for the Arctic fox, which is sacred to the Refurserkir and therefore eaten only by their initiates), the ormolu lichen is something of a staple. Though its medicinal benefits have yet to be studied in any extensive detail, the lichen is undoubtedly a neural stimulant far superi-

sold. This is so much cooler than caffeine."

Her mood seemed to have shifted, though I wasn't sure why. She was just more withdrawn all of the sudden and she wouldn't meet my eyes with hers.

"To tell you the truth," she said, "I was just trying to disorient you a little. I wanted to catch you off guard. In case you actually had followed me here. You'll get used to it."

"Wow. Subterfuge... Heh. Centrifuge... Is there such a thing as subterfugal force?"

"There's no such thing as centrifugal force."

"Really? Because I'm pretty sure that I've heard of something like that." I started trying to think back to physics class in high school, but then I suddenly wasn't sure if I'd ever taken a physics class.

"I'm sure you've heard of centrifugal force," the woman said, "but it's just a fiction... Imaginary, though we can nonetheless feel its effects, pulling us away from the people and things that we revolve around."

"Huh. Probably not, then. And what would it do, anyway?"

"I'm afraid that I'm completely unable to follow the meanderings of your thought."

---

or to ginseng or gingko biloba, and the clarity of vision attained by a diet consisting solely of this marvelous manna-like substance was the direct source of Jorgen's inspiration for his brilliant but doomed proposal of a rhizomatic replacement of the Dewey Decimal System. From an unpublished interview: "In Vanaheim, the World Tree of mainstream Norse mythology has been supplanted by the lichenous World Rhizome, binding the Nine Worlds together without hierarchy... just as familial relations, there, are also non-linear—or extensive, rather, along all possible lines of flight, each node bound to each other in an infinite skein of interconnections. Such is the library I envision; such is the library in my mind."

"Oh yeah! Why exactly do you think people are following you?"

"I'm probably just paranoid."

"Oh. I still don't understand, though."

"I didn't mean you to."

"Oh."

"I will explain. Just give me a minute. I think I've decided that I want to tell you. I'm trying to work up the nerve... You don't mind, do you?"

"I don't think so."

"Good. Sometimes it's just easier to talk to strangers, you know."

"For the first time in a while, I understand exactly what you're saying," I told her. But if I knew what I meant when I said that, it must have immediately slipped my mind.

WIBLE & PACHECO

Immediately upon ascertaining that Our Heroine was no longer surveilling us, we returned via circuitous route to the house of Hubert Jorgen. To our disappointment, we found the windows of the ground floor to be more securely fastened than those of Our Heroine's house had been. We were thus forced to resort to a greater degree of skullduggery in order to gain our entry.

Mr. Pacheco removed pick and torque wrench from an interior pocket of his overcoat and applied them to the simple lock of the front door handle while Mr. Wible stood watch upon the stoop. He noted no passersby. Most likely he was too busy fussing with his pipe to note much of anything.

Luckily for Mr. Pacheco—whose lock-picking skills could

generously be described as meager—the deadbolt had not been turned, and after a few minutes of tinkering he managed to open the door. We took care to close and lock it securely behind us.

Our proof was approaching its logical completion. Though still lacking support for a few of our assumptions, and though the clues we had amassed might not have been apparent to the casual observer, we were nonetheless confident that all would be confirmed once we had explored Hubert Jorgen's house in its entirety. Our intuition had led us in this direction from the beginning, and no datum to the contrary had yet arisen to dissuade us; the further we followed the clew of evidence, the clearer it became that our solution was the only one possible to the unstated riddle that we sought to solve.

The clew of evidence was leading us now to the bedroom. The most intimate of chambers, we reasoned that it was therefore the likeliest in which to discover hidden things. We assumed that it lay on the second floor, and the stairs—white and spiral—led directly up from the foyer. As we set our feet upon the first step, however, we heard a familiar noise emanating from a room immediately adjacent.

Rather, more precisely, we recognized the lack of any noise at all emanating from the room—as one might notice the left or right channel's absence from a familiar stereophonic recording. We delayed our ascent.

"We have heard nothing like this before," Mr. Wible whispered.

"So I recall," Mr. Pacheco answered in a similarly quiet voice. "We heard nothing like it during our first collaboration with the Bean-Ymirsons."

"Then you agree with me as to what it portends?"

"I do."

We were not afraid. Rather, we were both agreed that our investigation must continue, regardless of the cost. With all of the gentleness that we were capable of mustering, then, we stepped down from the stair and moved in the direction of the room from which the noise did not emanate. Mr. Pacheco rummaged through his pockets for anything that might be used as a weapon, but the search was fruitless. Mr. Wible did not even try.

Though we crept up to the door slowly, we opened it quickly, so as not to allow the escape of whomever—or whatever—lurked behind it. Mr. Pacheco, however, spoiled any real chance of surprise by failing to contain a slight yelp just prior to our ingress. When Mr. Wible opened his eyes and emerged from behind Mr. Pacheco, of course, he saw that the room contained no immediate threats. Surprise, therefore, was not a relevant issue.

The general appearance was that of a dining room. A bowl of plastic fruit sat on a large octagonal table, which, in its turn, rested on a brightly colored rug of Turkmenistanish design that covered most of the tile floor. We noticed that the table's oak veneer was covered in a thin patina of dust; no meals had been served thereon for many days.

Mr. Wible began to speak, but Mr. Pacheco placed an admonishing finger first to his lips and then pointed it in the direction of a closed door on the dining room's far end. We could hear nothing happening on the other side; again with speed and stealth, we pressed onward, deeper into the house.

The kitchen, like the dining room before it, was seemingly devoid of occupants. Dishes were in the sink, however, and we could now hear the slow drip of the tap upon the backside of a frying pan. Someone had cooked an egg breakfast approximately ten hours earlier. No. Correction: Someone had cooked a breakfast of egg-*fakes* approximately ten hours earlier. The theme of forgery ran strongly within this house.[37]

"Shh," Mr. Pacheco said. We stood still for a moment. We could also now hear the thrum of the refrigerator. The sound of nothing was now elsewhere.

Mr. Pacheco removed a small magnet in the shape of an Arctic fox from the freezer door. "Perhaps we should leave," he suggested quietly. "If we are correct in our assessment of the current situation, we will most likely face some difficulty in executing a full search of the house at this time."

"Perhaps," Mr. Wible answered. "But there is also the possibility that we are being overly cautious and that delay could cost us the chance of achieving our goal. It is difficult to say with certainty whether the silences that we were noticing truly had the same quality as those which we last encountered over twenty years in the past, or if it is only that our senses are dulling as we approach old age."

Mr. Pacheco returned the magnet to the freezer door.

"Let us continue our search, then," he said.

We headed back through the dining room to the foyer.

"Shall we still begin in the bedroom?" Mr. Pacheco asked.

He did not hear the response of Mr. Wible behind him.

---

37. Hubert Jorgen in conversation: "Forgery, I think, is perhaps the pinnacle of self-expression, paradoxical as it sounds. There's a school of thought that says the more constraints put upon a piece of art—rhyme and meter, say, in the case of poetry, or photo-realism in the case of painting—the more impressive that artwork is if executed successfully. Well, what could be more constraining than forgery? And if you manage yet to express yourself within that rigorous framework, what, then, could be more impressive?"

"What am I doing?" I asked myself aloud, but I couldn't think of a good response.

I used my boots to clear away some snow and sat down on the curb of Skellington Road. My cheeks grew instantly cold. I could hear the throb of blood in my temples. I could see the steam falling out of my mouth as I spoke.

"Damnation!"

It was going to get dark soon.

My hands, at least, were warmish in their gloves. I held them palm up in front of me to let some snowflakes collect. The white shapes stood out clear and definite against the glove-black. Stupid Wible and Pacheco connect-the-dots dumbness. Implying that Shirley, Hubert, and I were all dots in the same line.

"I am not a detective."

I was not.

But things were occurring to me, nonetheless.

When I was younger the world shone brighter and definite. Moments of eidetic clarity and purpose, patches of time more vibrant for their flickering on the edge of death's black opacity. Like nearly freezing with Prescott in a quasi-iglooesque enclosure in glacial Greenland, groping, crowded close to a pile of antiquities we'd barely managed to ignite—my mother would have rather died—biting the frost from each other's faces and inhaling deeply to capture each calorie that passed between us through breathsteam. The memory so sharp of walls melting down around and smoke choking despite the makeshift chimney. The fire was almost too bright to stare into. When we ran out of what we thought were medieval "pieces of the true cross" (but which were merely 1950s forgeries, we found out later), we threw on clumps of leaves from my teenage diaries. Momentary kindlings, brief semblances of blaze as my adolescent cravings crumpled, blackened, to ash... No passion that burned consistently toward anything, anyway. Then, all that was left, little embers glowing weakly in the center of our translucent ice tomb. Not even enough to cast a shadow. Too many times we almost died, though, together... Tricking us into intimacy. And all the attendant excitement, the suspense of not really knowing whether we'd really pull through this time... Or some other excuse.

Everything around me, now, was white. Even the house across the street. Of course the snow, but I imagined myself as if from above, and I was the only thing of any color in the scene at all. Like Prescott after the avalanche, lying there in imitation of a Pepsi logo. The bright blue of his parka, the white of the snow, the red of his blood...

It was good that he was gone. Connie was right. But that didn't mean he'd had to go.

Back to Gerd.

I silently prayed that Gerd wasn't involved in this.

I didn't mean to make sense of things. My mind just naturally worked that way.

"Where is Garm?" I said aloud in a futile effort to distract myself. I stood up and stretched out and tried to rub my cheeks awake. Sitting had been stupid. I'd just have to go home and wait. I'd never find him, looking. I should have just posted flyers in the first place, but it was getting too late for that now.

Maybe Hubert would call again, though. Maybe he'd

explain everything, tell me I was paranoid. Or Nathan. Maybe they already had called. I just hoped Constance hadn't been the one to answer.

CONSTANCE

Pausing for a moment to listen, on my way back down the spiral staircase, I could just barely discern the ringing of the telephone. I deduced that it must have been filtering up through some inconspicuous vent that I was unable to locate in the candlelight. If it was Our Heroine, I would just have to tell her when she got home that I'd been unsure whether I should answer it or not, this not being my house and I not being such an inquisitive person that I would stoop to intercepting phone calls obviously not meant for my ears. Or something to that effect.

I halfway hoped it was her, however, since that would indicate that she wasn't about to burst in and discover me. But I was almost home free, now, anyhow. My prize in one hand, my candle in the other. I wrote the headline in my mind: "Final Manuscript of Shirley MacGuffin, Found in Our Heroine's Secret Hideout!"[38]

It only struck me when I was about three-quarters of the way down that there should have been more light. I had left the door open, hadn't I? Of course I had; I didn't even know

38. The second of the three semi-significant absences that I noted earlier, I am confounded by the lack of any narrative description of what exactly Constance Lingus found at the top of the stairs. One must suppose that these are the pages on which she eventually based the famous article that made so many tasteless claims against the by-then recently deceased Valison. Which, even if it was based in any sort of fact, doesn't make it any less tasteless.

how to close it. But reaching the bottom only confirmed my fear. The entrance actually *had* slid somehow shut behind me.

Trapped! Well, was this to be the end of Constance Lingus, then? Ridiculous. Surely there must be some hidden switch or something, I reasoned. You can't just go making secret passages that don't open from the inside. I held the candle up to the seemingly smooth wall in front of me for a closer look. Wax dripped down off of it to the tender spot where thumb meets index, but my fierce tenacity allowed me to keep hold. I now noticed, however, that the candle had burned down to about a quarter-stick. There wouldn't be much light left. I figured that I'd better just look fast.

BLAISE

Through the window of the staircase landing, I notice that the sun is about to set. I cannot see the sun itself, but the grayish white of the western sky has begun to yield to a darkness that spreads downward from the zenith, descending with the snow.

Electricity is another of the amenities in which the Two-Story House is lacking, and—considering the imminent arrival of night—I realize that I must either conclude my search soon or adjourn it in favor of finding a flashlight. With tired body and tired mind, I continue up the stairs.

The room that exists directly at the staircase top is little more than a wide, empty hallway, dimly lit by a translucent skylight. Three doors—all closed—lead from the room, and each of them is blanketed in Shirley's sentences. I notice immediately that a further textual complication is introduced on this level of the house; the narrative voices have switched to the first-person. This is encouraging, however, for that is the person of the sentence I seek, from her journals, to find its context: *I am a fish*.

My vision is blurred with the strain of undersleep and too much caffeine, but I only rub my eyes and read on.

The leftmost door contains such sentences as "(Red) I rattled the knob and kicked the door, so rudely forced," "(Green) I leaned my head against the door and just stood there for a moment, breathing," and "(Blue) 'I'm so sorry,' I said."

Despite the added confusion that stems from indeterminate speakers, I believe that I am becoming able—by application of my husbandly knowledge—to make distinctions between the two stories. For instance, Shirley would not write such blatant violence as door-kicking into the murder mystery, and she would particularly not write it in connection with the death scene. And that is the scene for which I search. So knowing that the scene will not be found here—and having little time left to read anything at all—I move on to the middle door.

Written upon this one, I find "(Yellow) I closed the door quietly behind myself," "(Yellow) From the hallway I could hear something in the room that sounded like a music box, tinkling its way through a tune that seemed almost familiar," "(Yellow) 'Are you okay in there?' I called through the door," and other sentences almost all of which are yellow.

This is not the death room, either. Though the mundane actions related on the door's surface would at first seem a perfect counterpoint to violent happenings within—heightening drama through starkness of contrast—the sentences lack even hints of the passion that must accompany the killing. Additionally, the music box is just the sort of device that my wife would have used to prompt the psychological revelation which forms the climax of the other story. I turn, then, to the rightmost door.

"(Green) The knob was so cold it felt wet; or maybe it was just my clammy hands." "(Yellow) I hadn't even noticed that my thumb was still bleeding, smeared rusty on my forefinger, but the cut was still bright, pulsing out red from beneath the little gill-flap." Reading only these two sentences, I know this is the room. I am certain, and I place my hand upon the doorknob.

It is indeed cold, and I allow my hand to linger for a moment—contemplating how the sensation could be like wetness and considering what that wetness would be—before I turn it. In my mind the knob is solid water, and my hand feels swollen and full of blood upon it. I am clumsy as I fill it with my heat... When I do open the door, though, I open it slowly—not out of reluctance, but rather of a desire to listen to the friction of its hinges. It is good to hear a noise in this house that is not I.

The two windows of the room face to the east and to the north, and as my eyes adjust to the darkness, I realize that the evening has arrived.

The word in English has increased my affection for this time of the day, the Evening... As if it were a time for the evening of all imbalances that the day has carried with itself. It is a friendly hour for justice.

As my pupils find their proper balance with the darkness, I discern a manly shape curled upon the floor. The speed of my action blurs my perception.

I believe that I move across the room, and then I am on my knees, next to the bundle upon the floor. The bundle is a man, and it is Hubert Jorgen. His body. He does not move.

I am an inspector again in this moment, rather than a jealous husband, and I place my rough fingers on his throat for a pulse. I feel none. Neither is there any breath issuing from his mouth or nose, and his body has the coldness of death. I can find no marks of injury, however. His left hand clutches a cellular telephone.

My first thought is that I will be the suspect in this, too, and that I must do something to avert that suspicion, for if I am incarcerated then my wife's killer shall walk free. I must inform someone else of this development. Though I would prefer it, I realize that I cannot be alone in this.

Rising from the body, then, I rush down the stairs, across the living room, out the front door, through my backyard, and into the kitchen of my house. From there I dial Our Heroine's number.

After four rings, her answering machine picks up.

"I must speak with you," I say. "I have found Hubert Jorgen, as I told you that I would. However, I have found him dead. I apologize that I am not as adroit as you in delivering news of death, but my English always worsens when you are around to hear it. He is in the Two-Story House. Goodbye."

I hang up the telephone. I must head back to the Two-Story House. Perhaps the killer is still there, in another of the rooms. But the evening is here, indeed, and first I must find a flashlight.

WIBLE & PACHECO

The illusion of time is such that the passage between moments seems continuous. Yet, if "passage" (and, by extension, "motion") is to be taken as an apt metaphor with which to describe temporality, then some quantum moment must exist with only void between itself and the next moment—else Achilles will never catch the Tortoise. We found this hypothesis to hold true when—one moment—we stood at the bottom of Hubert Jorgen's staircase and—the next—we were tied to bedposts in an upstairs room with a woman whom we assumed to be Gerd standing above us, dressed in a long black robe and twirling a crescent-shaped knife. Between these two discrete and seemingly noncontiguous points in time, we experienced only a void with which even silence and darkness could not be equated.

NATHAN

Everything around us just had this weird lucidity to it, darkness and light creating this great detail in their contrast. The textures and little crevices of the cave walls were clearer and more intricate than I thought they should have been—like hair strands under a microscope—and the colors were a lot more vibrant, too, especially considering that only green light was shining on them. I noticed now that the lichen was glowing more brightly than it had been before.

"Are you feeling all right?" the woman asked.

"Yeah. No problem. Are my pupils big, too?"

"Excuse me?"

"Well, I was just noticing how bright and clear everything

looks, and your pupils are pretty dilated... So I thought it might explain things if mine were, too."

"Oh. Yes, they are rather large. Another effect of the lichen, I'm postulating."

"Cool. I really dig this stuff." I poked an underwater patch of it with my forefinger. It wasn't as squishy as I thought it would be. "I didn't even know lichen could grow underwater..."

"Okay," she said. "I think I'm ready."

"To tell me what your problem is?" I asked. "Are you pregnant?"

"Am I— No! At least I hope not. Why would you say that?"

"I was just trying to guess. You know. That might be considered a problem, and it's something you might not want to talk about with people that you know. So were you raped?"

"I— Where are you getting this?"

"I don't know," I said. "I think I'm just smart. I keep having all these ideas. I'm a writer, you know."

She looked at me for a long time before she spoke, and I started to feel uneasy, but then her voice sounded really nice when she did speak, so it was okay.

"Let me run a story idea by you," she said. "I'm a writer, too. So I want to hear your ideas on this subject."

"Okay, shoot," I said.

"There are two stories, actually, in the same space, with the same characters. Each story is written on the walls and objects inside a house, sentences taking their physical space from the place of action rather than from their temporal relations."

"That's weird," I said.

"Just let me finish before you give me your ideas."

"Sorry."

"So, one of the stories is a slow human drama, wherein a woman is raped but the man thinks it's consensual, and so—"

"This reminds me of a movie I was in," I interrupted. "It was all about different perceptions, and rape and stuff. It was pretty cool. It all took place in a single room and it was shot on digital video—it was an indie movie, you know, and—" but then I was cut off by a male voice that echoed through the cave.

"What are you doing here?"

I leaned my head backward to see behind me. It was the son.

"Um... We're just sitting around," I told him. He didn't look happy. He looked upside-down.

"But I told you to wait in the Thing Room!" His eyes were wide and shaky, like Peter Lorre in *Casablanca* when he's about to get caught. He looked pretty pissed.

"You should go," the woman whispered to me. She slunk down into the pool.

"But what about you?" I asked her.

"I'll be okay."

"What about your problem?"

"It'll be okay, too. I'll find someone else to tell. You should go catch that plane back to somewhere else entirely. Worry about your own problem."

Her eyebrows had the mischievous wrinkle again.

"You must come with me now," the son said.

I frowned up at him—though I suppose it looked like a smile from his angle—and then I turned over to lift myself out of the steam pool. "What about her?" I asked.

"Hey, don't drag me into this!" She widened her eyes at me.

"She is an honored guest here," the son told me. "But my father did great amounts of niggling to gain your entrance... And you should not frown at me, but you should frown at yourself, for it is you who caused this trouble."

I was trying to pull my thermals on over my wet body, now, and I could tell that I was going to be cold quite soon.

"It is for your own good that I found you when I did," the son continued as I wormed my way into my jeans. He kept tapping his foot, trying to look impatient. "You must understand that this pool is sacred to the Refurserkir."

"I'm sorry," I said. "I didn't know."

"And so you should be sorry. It does not matter what you did or did not know." He kept looking all around. I could tell now that he was more nervous than mad.

The woman was just sitting there not saying anything, but every time I glanced over at her she was smiling right back at me from beneath her mischievously wrinkled eyebrows. I knelt down to tie my bootlaces.

"Um... Well, good luck with whatever it is," I said to the woman.

"Yeah, you, too." She was still smiling, and I suddenly realized that I had no idea what it was that so amused her. And I didn't know what else to say, either.

I got up and followed the son out of the room, then, but I shot one last glance backward before we turned the corner. Steam had already obscured everything, and I couldn't even see where she was. "Thanks a lot for everything," I called out. I listened closely, but if she responded I couldn't hear.

"You must be quiet," the son muttered without turning. "The Refurserkir do not take kindly to trespassers."

WIBLE & PACHECO

"What are you doing here?" the woman asked us, stowing her crescent-shaped knife in some inner recess of her robes. She spoke with a stilted deliberateness.

"Please be more specific with your query. If you question the general significance of man's presence in the universal scheme of things, then we— aah!"

"Why are the two of you in this house, right now? For what reason are you in New Crúiskeen, today?"

"We are investigators. We—"

"And what are you currently investigating?"

"The case is the world. We merely— argh!"

"As you asked of me a moment ago, please be more specific."

"We are in search of certain... documents."

"And precisely what are these documents that you are in search of?"

"We cannot say with precision, but— urgh!"

"I urge you to make an attempt. I understand that precision may not be your dominant virtue, and you have my assurances that I take no pleasure in causing you pain. However, my attendants have been trained to note the slightest fluctuations in my mood and to respond accordingly; if you continue to frustrate me with your answers, I must warn you that they will be compelled to further vent that frustration. Now, I ask again: What are these documents that you search for?"

"*Hamlet*. We labor under the hypothesis that the object of our search is an attempt to re-create the *Hamlet* of Thomas Kyd. We are not entirely certain of this, but we— aiyee!"

"Forgive my attendants. They mistake my lack of comprehension for annoyance. But how is it possible that you do not know for certain the object of your own search? I suggest that you make your answer as comprehensive as possible, thus sparing all of us the pain that will undoubtedly accompany any necessary follow-up questions."

We preceded our response with groans of affirmation. "When first approached, we were given only the vaguest of instructions regarding sensitive documents that we would need to retrieve in the event of Shirley MacGuffin's death. During the course of our investigation, we discovered that she had been working for some time on an approximation of Thomas Kyd's hypothetical *Hamlet*, but that she was only recently nearing its completion. Our most sound hypothesis is that her drafts of this project constitute the object of our search."

"I see..." her voice seemed to convey some confusion and a great deal of dissatisfaction with our answer, though no physical agony ensued. "But you still have not answered my initial question. What led you here, to this house?"

"Of course. Please pardon us... We began this case under the assumption that Ms. MacGuffin was murdered by fanatical Shakespeareans fearful that the publication of her *Hamlet* would undermine the primacy of Shakespeare's text as one of the defining master narratives of the western world... Yet additional information that we have accrued suggests, perhaps, the opposite. It is now our belief that the murderer plans to pass off Ms. MacGuffin's version of the play as the authentic work of Thomas Kyd—rather than as a work of art in its own right—precisely in an attempt to dislodge Shakespeare from his throne atop the canon. We believe that she was killed in order to ensure her silence.

Hubert Jorgen is a well-known expert on the subject of forgery, and it is for that reason that we have come to his home. Additionally—"

"You search for a play, then? Is this something that you are certain of?"

"As we have already informed you, we are not certain in the least; it is merely our most sound hypothesis. Do you suggest that we should not search for a— ack!"

"You are to infer nothing from my questions! Do you understand? Answer me!"

Through aching larynxes, we answered. "We do. We understand."

"Good. You have given me much to think on. I shall leave you in the company of my attendants for a while longer to ensure that you have much to think on, as well. You will not see me again."

She turned and swept from the bedroom in one fluid motion. Typography cannot convey the essence of our subsequent screams.

OUR HEROINE

"What?" I yelled. "Where were you? What did I let you stay here for, anyway? God... How could you let this happen?"

"Now, I realize that this isn't doing much to assuage your feelings of masculine abandonment, and I'm truly sorry for that, but you must understand that this wasn't my fault; I was locked in the bathroom."

"You were locked *in* the bathroom? You do know that the bathroom door locks from the inside?"

"Yes, I admit it's curious, but I just couldn't get it open. It was stuck, somehow. In fact, as I'm certain you'll notice, I eventually had to remove the—"

"Forget it. Just tell me what happened."

"All right. From the beginning, then... Hmm. I was sitting in the study, typing up my notes, musing over the best way to phrase a particularly poignant clause. But then my contemplation was suddenly disrupted by a far off ringing... It was the doorbell, I realized, and so I—"

"Let me see your notes."

"Excuse me?"

"You say you were typing them up, so I want to see what you typed. Is that it?" A thick sheaf of papers was protruding from her purse upon the couch.

"No!" Connie leapt in front of me before I could even begin to move couchward; she snatched up the purse and clutched it tightly to her chest. I didn't recognize the papers at the time, but perhaps that was for the best.

"I promise to let you preview any article before I publish it," she sputtered, "but I just have a complex about allowing people to see drafts of my work before I've had a chance to revise. I didn't actually get very much typed, anyway; it takes me some time just to get the gears turning, you see, and—"

"Never mind." I let myself collapse into the armchair by the coffee table, and Connie took the couch. "So, the doorbell rang..."

"Yes." She allowed herself to exhale. "So. On the other side of the door stood a man... He was probably in his early sixties, his face centered around an improbably big and bulbous nose... He claimed that he was here to see you. I assumed that he was expected. Lorenz, I believe he said his name was."

"And where is he now?"

"That's another thing I don't know, I'm afraid. But if you'd just stop interrupting me, I'd get to that."

"Fine. Go on."

"Okay. So, perhaps naively, I invited this man with the protuberant proboscis into your house. He seemed interested in speaking to your father—who had recently awoken and whom I was having a great deal of trouble in getting back to bed—so I showed him into the living room, here, and then went myself into the kitchen to put some water on for tea... Oh, I think I ruined one of your pots, by the way."

"That's really the least of my worries right now, Connie."

"Right. Of course. Well, I'd just started the water when—out of nowhere—I had to go to the bathroom. I'll spare you the juicy details. But, while I was *in medias res*, I heard the ringing of the telephone. Well, what exactly could I do in such a unfortunate situation? I hastened to finish up as quickly as I could, but before I was even in a state to think about pulling paper off the roll to properly wipe, the sound had ceased. I swear it wasn't more than two or three rings... Still, it was a relief, to me, at any rate. Since I'd missed it, I assumed that I could return to a more leisurely pace of things with regard to my toiletries... Of course, hardly a minute later, I heard the phone's clamorous ring again—and this led me to believe that whatever the matter was must be rather urgent—so I redoubled my bowel-evacuating efforts, and—"

"I thought you said you'd spare me the details."

"Yes, sorry. Well, I'm quite sure that I would have caught this second call in time, but when finally I flushed, I arose to find myself locked in. Trapped! The door mysteriously jammed, as I've already explained... And I could have sworn that I heard the answering machine pick the call up this time, but—as you can see for yourself—there are no new messages. I'm assuming that Lorenz fellow must have deleted it, though I have no idea why he'd do such a thing."

"And you couldn't hear who it was?"

"Well, actually... if I had to guess, I'd say it was Blaise Duplain. It did sound like his voice. But I couldn't swear to it. By this point the kettle was whistling rather fiercely, and I was having difficulty discerning even the sound of my own breath over its infernal howl."

"All right, fine. So then what happened?"

"Well, there isn't much left to tell, is there? I spent the next fifteen minutes or so banging on the bathroom door and otherwise attempting to extricate myself, but neither your father nor your large-nosed friend came to my aid... And it was only about fifteen minutes prior to your own arrival that I finally managed to get the knob off. So—"

"I see. And they were both just gone when you got out?"

"Exactly."

"I think I need to be alone now, Connie."

"I can help you."

"Yes, you can help me by leaving now."

After about half a minute of silence, she stood up. She didn't say anything, just stared at me for a second, sadly, then threw her purse over her shoulder and tromped toward the mudroom.

"I just want you to know," she said as she slipped into her shoes, "that though I may screw things up from time to time,

I am on your side. I didn't mean to lose your dad."

"Just go," I told her.

So she left, and my house was abruptly empty. I got up and glanced out the front window, but by the time I reached it she was already in the darkness, out of sight. Nighttime. Yet there were still a couple more hours to pass before I was supposed to be at Hrothgar's. In the quiet, in my empty house, I couldn't think of any way to occupy all that time.

Hours, with nothing to do but think, and things were beginning to come together, unbidden, in my mind. Lorenz must have left with my father. But why? And why was he invited to this get-together at Hrothgar's? He certainly hadn't seemed to know Shirley. Who else was supposed to be there? What had Leshio said? Angus, Leshio, Lorenz... "Mutt" Sanders? The former two both had an interest in Shirley's literary career. Which brought things back to *Hamlet*. And Hubert. One partial solution did occur to me, though I couldn't be certain of it; I wanted to believe I was just being paranoid. But then—if my partial solution was right—I'd be needing all the paranoia I could get. I tried not to think about it.

I did not want this, any of this—to be involved in it. I did not want to have anything to do with it. I did not want it, but now I had it anyway. What stone had I moved, like the famous Icelander, and across what road? And what could I do to put it back?

Never mind. Now, it was time to change. It was time to garb myself in nicer clothes and prepare for the night to come.

ICELANDER

CLUEDO

CHAPTER ONE

I arrived at Hrothgar's Mead Hall well before eight o'clock, weary of waiting around at home after a day of achieving nothing. I wanted to get a few drinks down before anyone else showed up. Outside, the snowfall had finally ceased.[39]

Hrothgar's was huge, as was everything in it. A central pillar carved from a single massive trunk of ash, banquet tables running the length of the floor. The bar itself was about twelve

39. Compare the initial lines of Valison's *The Fox in the Snow* for an example of how the delivery of such simple information could be made elegant and compelling: "Snow has fallen until it can fall no more; the final few flakes settle into their heaps as exhausted clouds roll away in retreat—the overcast gray surrendering at last to night's darkened blue—thus ending this war between the states of sky." Yet such lack of artistic concern is perhaps appropriate, here, considering the sudden swerve of the text into the close first-person narration of Our Heroine, who always claimed to resent the "artificial means" through which Valison transformed her mother's diaries into textual masterpieces. Yet even she must admit that art and artifice are inextricably linked.

yards long, polished rosewood, and there was a tap for each foot of it. Despite such length, every stool was filled; the locals made a point of arriving early on Bean Day to assert their proprietary claim.

The high wooden walls of the place were hung with chalk drawings that depicted the logos of the various available beers. This month's guest brew was St. George's Winter Ale, and its logo showed the eponymous saint lounging beneath an apple tree while some sort of dew—presumably Winter Ale—dripped from the fruit and into his yawning mouth. In the background, a white-clad damsel was battling a dragon; she used a hairbrush instead of a sword.

I found myself a place at the bar-end of one of the banquet tables, next to the stage, and draped my jacket around the ladder-backed chair. Despite how busy it was in here, a waitress appeared at my side almost immediately. Though she was tall, skinny, and blond—and therefore difficult to distinguish from any other waitress who had ever worked at Hrothgar's—I thought that she might be new. She patted all of her pockets before locating the pencil behind her ear.

"Hi, are you ready to order?"

"I'll wait, thanks," I said. "I'm meeting someone." I removed my gloves and stuffed them into a pocket of my coat behind me.

She whizzed away, then, and after I saw that she was safely in the backroom I got up and ordered myself a pitcher of Heidrun directly from the bartender. Perhaps I was being paranoid, but it was better than being unprepared. I returned to my seat before I poured the first honey-blond pint.

The bustle here tonight pleased me. The mass of people

would make it harder for anyone to try anything, if my paranoia proved well-founded. Students and townies alike crowded in for food, fire, and alcohol to ward away the cold; chatter in the background instead of music; waitresses billowing out of swinging doors, bearing with them whiffs of the fries and shepherd's pies that they carried upon their platters... Not quite authentic Nordic cuisine, but the aroma blended well with the general smell of spilt beer.

I was watching two blond busboys on the stage next to me setting up the microphone, video monitor, and song-machine—their musculature was of the wrong tone for Refurserkir—when the waitress returned and eyed my pitcher with a look of slight puzzlement.

"Still waiting?" she asked.

"Indeed," I said.

As she rushed away again, I took a little sip of my beer. It tasted normal enough. So a long swallow, then. Inoculation against the cold, and when I set the glass back down I'd drained a full third of it. I had to pour myself another only a few moments later.

I focused on the crispness of the beer's flavor, the bubbles rising up in it and the way that they caught the light and carried it to the snowy head.

I was dribbling the last suds out of the pitcher when Angus O'Malvins was just there, suddenly. Standing across the table and grinning down at me, one hand gripping the top rung of his chair while the other slipped his trademark Meerschaum pipe into an interior coat pocket.

"Hullo! An ah wis surtain ah'd be the first ane here," he said, his burr sounding thicker than ever.

"And I thought I'd have the place to myself for a while longer. But sit down, Mr. O'Malvins... I was just about to order another round."

"Ach, ye knae better than thah, poppet; yir ainly tae caw me Angus." He pulled the chair out and fussed his way down into it.

A few years had passed, now, since I'd seen any more of him than a picture on a Christmas card, but he looked almost exactly the same as when I'd first met him. A bushy white beard covered most of his face, and the rest was red, his cheeks pushing up to force his eyes into a permanent squint.

"You made it here rather quickly," I said. "Quite a trip from the Orkneys, isn't it?"

"Aye, well, luckily ah wis in London when ah heard, sae ah wis able tae get a quick flight."

"I see. So, who else did you say was coming?" I asked, trying not to meet his eye.

"Ach, whae isnae coming? E'en auld Magnus promised thah he'd pop in, though he somehoo seemed a bit reluctant."

"Yeah, that doesn't surprise me. I don't think he's ever been here, even though he lives just around the block. Too popular for his taste, I'd imagine."

"Hmm, aye, he *can* act the part of the elitist, noo... But sae, then, there's alsae 'Mutt' Sanders, whae ah dinnae believe ye knae... an Philip Leshio, the auld bore, whae, ah believe, ye unfortunately dae knae. Dr. Albertine, alsae, an... Ach, Michael Lorenz, whae—as ye can or cannae know—is a visiting professor this semester at yir ain university."

"Actually, I met him earlier today. He seemed... interesting. But I didn't know that he knew you or Shirley."

"Michael? Well, we've a few acquaintances in common, but—"

The waitress finally returned.

"Ready for a refill?" she asked, picking up the empty pitcher.

"Please. And a glass for my friend."

"On its way." And off she went again.

"But jist whit sort ay shenanigans have ye been up tae yirself thir past few years?" Angus asked. "Done any scribbling tae mention?"

"Oh... I haven't been up to much. All I've written recently are academic articles. Shirley was working on a few things, though. In fact, I thought she might actually get something published soon."

I watched his face for a reaction, but he remained squint-eyed and smiling.

"Truly?" he asked. "Ah hadnae any idea."

"Yeah, well, it's interesting, actually—"

"And here you go." The waitress poured a glass for Angus and then set the second pitcher on the table. "Are you still waiting for more people before you order?"

"We are, thank ye," Angus replied.

When she walked away again, he lifted the pitcher to freshen my glass.

"Sae, Shirley's impending publication," he said, pouring directly into the glass's bottom, and half the beer bubbled into head. "Ah suppose thah yir referring tae thah faux-Shakespearean idea she had, then?"

I didn't immediately respond. Stageward motion had caught my eye as he spoke, and I turned to watch; the busboys were finished setting up, and Roger Harrod—the owner of Hrothgar's—was getting ready to speak.

"Have you ever been here for a karaoke night before?" I asked, turning back to Angus. "Looks like it's about to start. I think you'll like it."

"Karaoke? It isnae really ma—"

"Hrothgar's puts a unique spin on things," I said, cutting him off. "They call it skaldic karaoke."

"An whit the divil is thah?"

"Well, basically it means that all of the songs are heroic ballads, as opposed to your usual pop hits. It's almost eight o'clock, though. Where's everybody else? They'll miss all the fun."

"Ach, dinnae worry. Ah'm sure they'll be here shortly."

"Okay, everybody... Here we go," Roger said from the stage, swirling pieces of paper around in a bowl with his fingertips before closing his eyes and drawing one out. "It looks like the first skald of this evening, folks... is going to be... Mr. Jim Bliss! And he'll be singing the ballad of Liutbold the Kind. Come on up here, Jim, and show us what you're made of!"

A lanky, bespectacled fellow in a brown suit and matching bow tie stood measuredly from his seat across the room and proceeded to bump and pardon his way stageward.

"Sorry," he said as he passed our table, though he didn't seem to touch either one of us. Ignoring the stairs at either stage-end, he clambered directly up the front, his brown trousers gaining gray swathes of dirt across the knees as he did so.

Roger patted him on the back and whispered something in his ear before taking a quick bow and hopping from the stage.

"Hello," the man mumbled in a strange accent; his voice was hardly audible though he bobbed his head toward the microphone as he spoke. "Er... Well, I suppose you can start the music now."

After a moment of quiet static crackle, a 2/4 drumbeat began to pulse from hidden speakers while the synthetic approximation of a plucked string instrument arpeggiated over it, back and forth between the dominant and tonic of some minor key. A faint trace of bass lingered thumping in the background, too, and—following a few introductory bars—the man joined his voice to it all in a startlingly strong tenor. Thus was Liutbold the Kind launched on his long journey through a day of strange synchronicities and personal revelations. Not the standard set of heroic deeds, but eccentricity was probably the ballad's greatest strength. Angus sat listening with cocked head and hanging jaw.

"It's wonderful," he whispered after a few reverent seconds.

"See, I thought you'd like it."

"Ah truly dae," he replied, reaching over the table as if to clap me on the shoulder, though I shied away enough that he couldn't quite reach me—I didn't feel like a shoulder clap just then. My unexpected movement threw him a bit off balance, and he almost knocked my beer over as his hand came down on the table. "Ah'm sorry ah doubted ye even fir an instant."

I saw that my glass was cold, still full, and wet with condensation, so I grabbed a handkerchief from my jacket behind me to wipe it down before I took a long draught.

"Back tae the subject ay Shirley's *Hamlet*, though," Angus said suddenly, though his eyes were still upon the stage. "Ah interrupted ye earlier; ye were saying aboot hoo she wis nearly done with it... Trying tae get it published, ah believe ye mentioned. But tell me everything. Did she ivir show ye her drafts?

An were they actually any guid?"

He wasn't going to let this go, I realized, and it was then that I began to believe my paranoid suspicions must indeed be correct. After a pause I answered him.

"All right, then," I said. "If you want to get right into it..." I suddenly noticed that I was really starting to feel a bit drunk, even though I'd only had four beers, which normally wouldn't have been nearly enough to buzz me.

"Is this a sore subject fir some reason? We are here tae discuss Shirley, are we nae?"

I sighed. He looked exactly the same as when I'd first seen him.

"All right," I answered, finally resigning myself. "I see you're ready, so let's just do this." I wanted to get this over with while I was still a little sober. "I never saw Shirley's version of Kyd's *Hamlet*," I told him.

The only complete piece of Shirley's work that I'd ever read, in fact, was an epic poem that she'd written in miniscule longhand across the sides of the stalls in the Hrothgar's ladies' room. It was called "The Hysteriad: A poem written by a woman, about women, and in a womanly space," and—according to Shirley—it was a reaction to the "oppressively masculine space" of Hrothgar's main dining hall, dominated as it was by the phallic central pillar and where not a single heroine could be found among the myriad heroes of the karaoke song-list.

She'd written the poem about four years earlier, which was impressive if only for the fact that Roger remained ignorant of its existence. Because he most definitely would have had it painted over if he'd heard even vague rumors of what it contained. But apparently no one had blabbed, since the poem was still there. It had grown, even, as four years worth of women had added their commentary between Shirley's widely spaced lines. Some of the comments were complimentary and others were critical, but I suspect that Shirley had been happy just to have started a dialogue.

It would be a betrayal of the poem to summarize its content outside of its context, but to say the least I was amazed. I hadn't expected to like it, but I did. I marveled at the musicality of it, as well as its humor and the depth of thought that it displayed. Somehow, before reading it, I'd always written Shirley off as untalented, solely on the basis of her self-admitted pretension. But the poem was actually good. The pretense was justified.

I, however, had come to the point where I couldn't justify my own pretense any longer.

"I never saw Shirley's version of Kyd's *Hamlet*," I told him. "She did, however, tell me a fair amount about the other one..."

"Other ane? Other whit? Other *Hamlet*?" he asked. "Ah cannae say ah'm at aw certain whit ye mean."

"You know exactly what I mean." Onstage, the singer had slipped out of his jacket and draped it over the song machine. He was just coming to the funeral sequence. "I really thought you were dead, you know, and so I figured that it couldn't be you. That you couldn't be him, and that it was safe to like you again... But what should I call you, now, anyway? I'm definitely not going to keep calling you Angus."

His face was contorted in an admirable display of confusion.

"Jist whit are ye driving at, poppet?" He said it softly, through the corner of his mouth. "Mist ye ay speak in riddles?

But we'll have nae more ay this 'Mr. O'Malvins' malarkey, if thah's whit yir suggesting; ah tellt ye earlier thah yir tae caw me Angus an nowt besides."

"No. I'm not going to give you the honor of that name anymore. I'm sorry, but I just never wanted to believe it was you."

"Ye nivir—" he began, turning his eyes to the stage.

"I mean, I guess some part of me has always known, sort of," I interrupted. "But I've always liked you when you called yourself Angus... What happened between you and Shirley in Denmark, though... I guess that's what finally made me—" I broke off mid-sentence and tried to focus on him through my bleary eyes. "I can't believe you could be so hideous!" I spat. "I can't believe that you could do that to her and then be so vain as to—"

His eyes remained on the stage.

"So I'm not going to call you Angus," I said, decisive. "The person I called Angus would never have done that. And he wouldn't have killed her just because... Why, because she confronted you about it and shattered your illusions that it was anything other than what it was?"

My eyes were already bleary from drunkenness, but now I was beginning to cry.

"You've given me a wide array of other names to choose from, though, haven't you?" I said. "Leshio and Lorenz, those were both you... And oh yeah—just who's this 'Mutt' Sanders, anyway?"

"You're starting to slur, my dear. Perhaps you had best—"

"Fine," I interrupted. "I suppose Surt will have to do, then."

He sighed. "Do you even appreciate the fact that I did this all for you?" he muttered, not looking at me. "Admittedly,

I also benefited; I haven't had a worthy adversary since your mother died. But you've been floundering, my dear. And I have given you meaning."

He watched the stage in silence for a few seconds longer, his jaw slack in the semblance of awe; when he turned to me, though, it was with his most malicious grin. His teeth were as white as snow, and he was just staring at me; it seemed like forever.

For a second, then, in his silence and the strangeness of everything, I forgot what we'd just been talking about. The singer had come to the tavern scene, now, and in order to describe the burly bartender he dipped into an implausibly resonant baritone. I was astounded at the transformation, and I turned to him, my blunted senses focused almost exclusively on the pleasurable vibration of my eardrums for the rest of that second. For the first time, I was really beginning to understand the appeal of this song. And then, in the next second, I was somewhere else entirely.

CHAPTER TWO

I thought that I might be unconscious but for the fact that I was thinking. Possibly just in darkness, then, and thinking unclearly. And silence, too. My senses were returning, but with no recollection of where they'd been. Between beer and here, Hrothgar's and now: only an instant.

A stench.

Not like rotten eggs or even sulphur. But methane, maybe. And the ammoniac tang of piss.

It was warm, as well, and I had a headache. In fact, it was hot.

Darkness, silence, odor, heat... The sewers, then? But my feet weren't wet. I noticed, then, that I was standing. I was still most likely underground, though, so probably the steam tunnels. My own bladder was quite full, but maybe bums pissing down here, methane leaking out of pipes, could account for... A working hypothesis, at least. But why no lights?

In the distance, maybe. I squinted. No lights apparent, but there was texture. There was distance. Must have been some light, then, somewhere. Something. And I could almost see it.

Shape and movement on the edge of sight...

Or just phosphene in my eyeballs?

Like breaking clouds. Rorschach. Horsehead. Seeing what I wanted to... But no. I felt certain that something solid lingered on the edge.

I'd been drugged, I realized.

But I was coming out of it now.

My awareness was expanding. Through my grogginess. My drunk and drugginess. Too rapidly, though. Like sudden adrenaline or caffeine. Milk in coffee unfurling. Clouds that break.

I felt slightly nauseated, and my mouth was dry and bitter.

How had he done it? I didn't let the new waitress bring me my beer. I avoided his shoulder clap... And he'd slipped it in my beer as his hand came down to the table, I realized. Then he'd dragged me here. But where was here? And when?

I was able to turn my head. At every angle, though, only the same insensible scene, so I had nothing to judge by.

I was able to turn my head, but I could hardly shake my bloodless hands stuck up above it or lift my tingling legs. Thin leather straps attaching me to pipes behind. Itchy and damp on my wrists, but mostly from my own sweat. It was very hot. I was wearing my jacket.

Definitely the steam tunnels.

My headache eased a bit further away from me, then,

and my heart started pumping faster. I took a deep breath and tried to slow it down.

I was fully awake, now, at least. More than fully, and I squinted again—tried to focus—peering hard into the darkness, as if it were a veil and I could see through its weave... But it wasn't. I still couldn't see a thing.

I did feel the movement, though. The sense of it. Something out there aside from eye-floaters.

"Hello?" I called.

Only my own echo. Sharp. Against concrete walls and copper pipes. Not a very large room. Ten by ten, maybe...

But where was he? I'd forgotten how annoying being tied up could be.

At least I was safe. He wasn't going to kill me. He could have buried me alive in the graveyard instead of bringing me here. Poisoned me in the bar instead of drugging me. So I was safe. Because he would have if he were going to. He just left me here in the dark to scare me...

I'd been afraid of the dark, once. But it had been so much worse when my mother had lit the acetylene torch and I'd actually seen the guy's misshapen face... Now I was just bored of the dark.

And silence.

Like a pale heart-shape in the blackness, then—spectral—resolving into a face as my pupils opened farther. And white hands, but with nothing in between. My pupils couldn't open any more.

I wasn't scared.

I did let out a little exclamation, though, and my bladder was beginning to hurt. And then I spoke. I don't know why.

And I don't know why I said the words I said, particularly. Just to say something, I suppose, in the silence. They meant nothing at all. But it was what I said:

"God... Mom."

And the movement came closer. It responded.

"Well... I'm not your mother."

Into range of the meager, sourceless light. Her white face framed in black. Black hair. Black robe. And I knew the voice.

"Gerd," I said.

She carried a stubby candle on a silver tray and lit it now with a silver cigarette lighter. It flared up fairly strong, but I must have been wrong about the presence of methane; she set the candle down on a foldout card table in the corner to my right, and when she turned around, she was smiling.

"So..." she said, looking me over as she secreted the cigarette lighter somewhere within the inner recesses of her robes. "Your roots are beginning to show. But otherwise, how's it going?"

I considered the question and looked around the room. It was a little bigger than I'd thought, exits leading out along either end of the wall to my left, which—along with the other walls—was lined with elaborate pipe work.

"Not so bad," I answered, eventually. "In fact, despite being knocked out and tied up, I'm feeling inexplicably euphoric. Fluid thoughts, vivid perceptions... Bitter back-taste on my tongue. I'm assuming you forced some extremely concentrated ormolu tea down my throat while I was unconscious?"

"Yes, so your powers of deduction have not abandoned you. I did indeed make you to drink ormolu tea, as it was the only means I could think of by which to revive you. But I can't say I'm very pleased to see you."

"Look, Gerd, I swear that I'm not investigating anything, if that's what this is all about."

"I had nothing to do with this," she said. "You were brought down here without my knowledge, in fact. Surt occasionally forgets that he answers to *me* on these matters and not to your ex-husband."

"You're saying that having me dragged down here was partially Prescott's idea?"

"Yes, well, Freysgoð[40] can be quite immature, as I'm sure you're aware. You're only fortunate that I was informed of your arrival before he was."

"No offense, but I think I'd rather deal with him."

"And I think that you'd be surprised by how much he's changed over the past few months... I doubt you'd even believe me were I to tell you what he's doing right now."

I didn't respond. I closed my eyes as sweat slid down across the left lid.

"Personally, you know, I'd hoped to leave you out of this." She let out a little laugh. "It's all so ridiculous. I mean, dragging you down here, you're just bound to piece things together... Unless we kill you, of course, but you know that I've never been a savage."

"Well, then, I guess I can only hope that you haven't changed as much as you say Prescott has."

"His name is Freysgoð."

"Whatever."

"No. Not whatever. I am serious on this point. His name

40. This term is actually a title denoting the earthly avatar of the god Frey. Prescott only took on the anglicized version of the name upon his adoption by the Bean-Ymirsons.

is Freysgo∂. Prescott was his name when he was yours, but now he is mine. The competition is over, and I have won. That is the reason I bear you no ill will."

"Well, that's all great... but I'm serious, too; whatever you want to call him, you can have him."

Her smile was hard to read in the candle-flicker, but after an abrupt intake of breath she said, "You cannot spoil my victory so easily. Though you may not speak it, nonetheless you know the truth."

"Okay, fine," I responded. "If it's what you need to hear, Freysgo∂ is yours. I lost him, through the mundanity of our marriage, and the fact that we had no real basis for a relationship to begin with. And you won him through the promise of a more exciting, fulfilling life. You're getting way too distracted by all of this, though... You were saying just a minute ago that you wished I'd never even been dragged down here, and I think that's a much more important topic than this one. Because I wish I'd never even been dragged down here, too... So, I mean, don't you think a nice solution for both of us would be to let me go?"

"Do not treat me as if I am an imbecile. If I let you go, what guarantee do I have that you will not just lead the police back down here?"

"What, lead them back down here to be slaughtered by your personal entourage? I don't think that would do any good for anybody. I didn't even know you were involved in this until you dragged me down here. Furthermore, I hardly even know what 'this' is, and I care about it even less. The only thing that I cared about at all was Shirley's murder, and I'm pretty sure you had nothing to do with that. Woman to woman, though,

I really need to use the ladies' room, so if you could just hurry your decision up a bit..."

Her punch was well placed, but I managed to hold everything in. She waited silently for me to open my eyes before she spoke.

"You are correct in assuming that I had nothing to do with the murder," she said.

"What was that you were telling me earlier about how you bear me no ill will?" I asked, still struggling back toward normal breathing.

"I do not. But that does not mean I will allow you to speak to me so insolently."

"I thought I was just being chummy."

She walked backward into the relative darkness for a moment but returned almost immediately, smiling brightly.

"Yes, you are right. We should be better friends. We have so much in common, after all. So be consoled with the fact that I do plan to cut you loose before Freysgoð gets here." She brandished a small, crescent-shaped knife that I assumed she must have pulled from somewhere within her robes. "But tell me first... Just how much do you know?"

"About what you and Surt are up to? Don't worry yourself about what I know. Because I don't *know* anything. Furthermore, I have almost no evidence to support any of my suspicions, and—as I said before—I don't really care whether you succeed or not. All I cared about was Shirley."

"Though you do not care, I would like you to indulge me nonetheless. In the spirit of our new friendship."

I noticed then the candlelight reflected in her eyes. Her irises were almost black. Suddenly her face seemed completely unfamiliar—just some other woman—and I couldn't recall why we'd always hated each other with such fervor. Something to do with Prescott, I supposed for a moment, but that seemed too simple...

And then it occurred to me what I must have represented to her; for the first time I actually *felt* it. Her entire way of life had been irrevocably altered when my parents exposed her society to the world at large. She had been meant to marry a living god, and that meaning had been taken away from her. Sure, my town may have been overrun by obsessive fans for one day a year, but her whole kingdom had been reduced to a tourist attraction. Perhaps it was just the ormolu tea messing with my mind, or the alcohol that was still in my system making me a sentimental drunk... But I decided, then, that I owed her *something*.

"Fine," I said. "I'll tell you what I think. But you'll need a little context first."

"I think we have time," she smiled.

"Okay," I said, nodding as much as I could from my trussed up position. "Three years ago, Shirley MacGuffin began working on a recreation of Thomas Kyd's *Hamlet*."

"Yes, that is what those two strange men said, as well, though I am unaware of this."

"You saw Wible and Pacheco?" I asked, but then I launched back into the story before she could answer and before my sympathy for her could be derailed. "So anyway, Shirley went to Denmark to do some research for the project, and while she was there she ran into her old friend Angus O'Malvins... Though I suppose I should call him Surt. But in the guise of Angus, he praised the ingenuity of Shirley's project but also suggested that it would be even more impressive if she could re-create the entire history of the character, beginning—and I'm guessing this was your idea—with a hypothetical Vanaheimic version of the story."

"I'm impressed. And this is all just speculation?"

"Well, call it inductive reasoning. She told me about her project, I knew Angus was in Denmark with her, and now I know that Angus was always just Surt in disguise. Seeing you here in New Crúiskeen and mixed up with him just completes the picture. But so your idea must have been that Shirley—talented as she was—would unwittingly create a text so plausible that it could be passed off as authentic if presented in the right format. With the help of an extremely talented forger,[41] then, and the right type of vellum..."

"Yes?"

"Well once you had a plausible forgery, I imagine you just planned to allow some anthropologist to 'discover' the sacred text that the Vanatru had been keeping safe for all of these years, thus instantly providing your country with an ersatz literary history of its own... A literary history which would, incidentally, establish Vanaheim as the originator of one of the central stories of Western literature, thereby advancing the state of its cultural legitimacy, furthering the cause of independence from Iceland, and... I don't know.[42] That's just about all I've got."

---

41. Fair enough, for once.

42. Were this indeed Gerd's project, what harm could have come from allowing its achievement? It would have been a victimless crime, if a crime it could be called at all. And how could anyone call it that when it would have done such a great good for such a great yet unheralded people? Is deception necessarily evil? I think not. I, at least, have nothing to be ashamed of.

"Ha! Well, I must applaud the precision of your 'inductive reasoning.' But what makes you so certain that I had nothing to do with the death of MacGuffin?"

"The thought crossed my mind, of course. But once you had your forgery, your main concern would just have to be the possibility that a copy of Shirley's original Vanaheimic text might still exist. Which is why you burnt down my father's library and broke into my house, etc. Just in case she'd given one of us a copy. But as long as there was no textual proof that Shirley had written the Vanaheimic *Hamlet* story herself, I think you'd have been content to let her make whatever claims she wanted. After all, what would be more plausible—the Vanatru actually possessing an ancient text of the Hamlet story or a writer whom no one had ever heard of claiming that she wrote it?"

"Well. Thank you," she said. It was almost a whisper.

"For what?" I asked.

"For presuming me to have common sense. For not thinking me to be nothing more than the villain of a mystery novel. All that I do, I do because I am concerned about the welfare of my people. I do not wish anyone to die unnecessarily. But who, do you suppose, did kill MacGuffin? Or, for that matter, who do you suppose killed your librarian friend?"

Her eyes were serious.

"Wait... What do you mean?" I asked.

"Jorgen, yes? His body was found by the Canadian inspector. It was not by my command. And that's really the extent of my knowledge on the subject."

"He's really dead?"

"Yes. It hardly matters, of course. Surt had a rather grisly fate in mind for Jorgen, regardless, and death is the only thing that saved him from it.[43] Surt did not inform me of precisely what his grudge against Jorgen was, but their partnership seems to have gone somehow sour."[44]

I didn't say anything for a moment, and Gerd just stood there twirling her little knife.

Their partnership?

"God," I said. "I'd really thought better of him, though..."[45]

"Ah. Indeed. So I've heard. Not your wisest choice, that."

Somehow, this was what made me lose my temper.

"Excuse me?" I said, looking back up and into her eyes. "I'm sorry, but I'm not about to start accepting relationship advice from Prescott's new girlfriend. Who also happens to be his half-sister, I might add, which is totally gross."

"His name is Freysgoð, and my relationship with him is none of your concern. Nor is he any of your concern." She wasn't

---

43. Of course, I had a suspicion of my own that strongly paralleled these lines of thought, but I have since come to revise my opinion. This could not have been true. She must have written all of this just to torment me with the slight possibility that these are, indeed, the Master's words. But I know better. Surt would not have questioned Jorgen's loyalty (had Jorgen been in some way complicit in Surt's hypothetical plot, that is—perhaps as Surt's handpicked successor. But this is a fact that I am in no way suggesting) unless someone had misled him, poisoning his mind against Jorgen. But Surt would not be so easily fooled. Hubert Jorgen's precautions must have been unnecessary—overkill. This cannot be the way it happened. I know this. Nothing can hurt me now.

44. Ha! Unless he was jealous. But, no, he would not be so petty.

45. Such coyness is one of the most infuriating aspects of this novel. That the Author would so strongly imply that Hubert Jorgen was somehow involved in the hypothetical forgery plot, tainting him with the guilt of the matter, yet refusing to commit wholly and describe the masterful skill—surpassing even that of Surt—with which Jorgen would have executed whatever part he might have played in such a plot had he been involved.

smiling now, but she was still spinning the knife, slowly, in her right hand. "He is not your husband any longer, and you will remember that in the future."

Then she grabbed my left hand with her own and drew the knife, quickly, straight through the base of my ring finger, then out the other side, just above the knuckle. I saw the finger hit the floor before I felt the pain.

"I'm going to cut you loose, now," she said, "as I promised that I would." She sliced with one motion through the left leather strap as she said it. "I am sorry about your finger, and I truly don't bear you any ill will." She cut the other strap just as easily as the first, and then the shape of her moved down to my feet; I couldn't quite make out any details through the blur of sudden tears.

"I've actually been thinking that we needed to talk about all of this for quite a while now," she said. "My only regret is that it had to happen under such unpleasant circumstances. Perhaps next time you're in Vanaheim we can continue this discussion in a more amiable manner. And I'll just hold on to your finger until then."

My feet were free, and I fell to the floor.

"Anyway, you should probably go now. Freysgoð is undoubtedly close to finished with your father, and I'm sure you'll want to be gone before he gets here. I'm afraid he won't be very pleased with me when he finds out that I've let you leave, of course, but then you don't need to worry about his moods anymore, do you? Although I suppose he might send the Refurserkir after you... So, on second thought, perhaps you do need to worry about just this one mood. But don't fret; I'll do my best to dissuade him."

I didn't say anything coherent—just staring down at the blurry hem of her robe, holding my left hand in my right—but she stood there, still for a moment in front of me, before moving toward the table to pick up the candle tray.

"Well, all right, then," she said. "It's been nice talking to you."

And then she blew out the watery candlelight and was gone.

After a short while, I was able to stand, and I stumbled toward the wall that had been to my left. Toward where I recalled the wall having been, though I underestimated by a couple of feet—tripped before slamming my right hand against a pipe. The metal was hot, and I pulled immediately away.

I wasn't sure which direction Gerd had gone, or I would have taken the opposite. In my ignorance, I just settled on the direction that had originally been in front of me; I figured that there had to be an exit either way. I felt much more comfortable after I took a moment to squat. I walked quickly, then, and I tried not to touch the walls; my hands hurt enough already as it was.

I tried not to think about what Prescott was almost finished doing to my father.

On an average walk down New Crúiskeen streets, steam seemed to rise from the sidewalk just about every twenty feet. I was now in the place that the steam came from; this should have meant grates somewhere nearby for me to find... Light leaking in. Ladders leading upward. But after a minute or more of walking straight I still didn't see a thing. I did hear something, though, suddenly behind me, and—pivoting on one heel—I screamed something back.

A voice whispered my name. A male voice, familiar, and it sounded about ten feet away.

"Prescott?" I called, tentatively.

"No. It's Nathan," the voice stage-whispered back. "I met you earlier, remember? You don't happen to have a light, do you?"

"Nathan! God, you scared the—" I let out the deep breath I'd taken, but it didn't really relieve my frustration.

"Sorry," he answered, still quiet, coming closer. "You don't happen to know the way out of here, do you?"

"No," I said. "I have no light. I don't know the way out."

"Just checking."

I could almost make out the shape of him, standing there, holding his own shoulder. A solid silhouette against the otherwise nebulous black.

"What are you doing down here, anyway?" I asked. "Are you okay?"

"I was looking for you, actually."

"And you knew I'd be down here?"

"Well, it's kind of a long story. And I think we should probably try to be quiet until we know that we're safe." He lowered his voice back to a whisper. "For now why don't we just concentrate on finding our way back to the surface?"

This made sense, I supposed. Just in case the Refurserkir really were after us.

"Okay," I said. "Except for the fact that neither one of us has any idea which way the surface is."

"Sure we do," he replied. "Up."

CHAPTER THREE

Nathan's response wasn't quite as inane as it sounded. What I'd failed to notice in my attempts to avoid touching the pipe-lined wall was that side passages occasionally branched off at inclines and declines from the tunnel that we were in. Nathan had joined my passage from one of the declines, though he'd gone up and down a few times before reaching me and wasn't certain which level he'd started on. Taking inclines whenever we could, though—over the next several minutes—we managed to make our way to a tunnel with grates letting out directly onto the world above. What I assumed were streetlamps filtered down through them, and I could make Nathan out a little more clearly. Enough to know that it was really him. Still holding his shoulder.

"I could give you a boost," he said. "Maybe we can reach one of those grates."

"It's too high," I answered. "Let's just see if we can find a grate with a ladder." I started off in a direction at random and he trotted after me.

"What are these tunnels here for, anyway?" he asked.

"I'm not sure, exactly. But I know the campus heating system is connected to them, somehow."

"Well, do you have any idea how far they extend horizontally? I mean, since they have something to do with the campus heating system, can we at least assume that we're beneath the campus?"

"I really have no idea," I said. "The power plant that provides the steam in the first place is kind of on the edge of town, so the tunnels are probably pretty extensive. I think the tunnels might have been here before the steam pipes, actually, though I don't really know the history that well."

The throb in my finger was getting worse, and I wanted to get out of there before the Refurserkir arrived. The throb where my finger had been. God. I was starting to feel a little lightheaded, too. Probably just the drugs and alcohol kicking back in, the ormolu wearing off. But what if I was losing too much blood? We had to get out of here.

"You know," I said suddenly, "I've heard legends about these tunnels—about kids getting disintegrated in bursts of steam... And I don't bring that up to scare you, but because I just recalled that all those legends mention ladders. Like a lot of ladders. It's supposed to be really easy to get out of here—in case an accident actually does happen—but in the stories the students are always just about to escape when the steam melts the flesh from their bones, and then some tunnel worker finds the skeletal remains still clinging to the ladder's top rung three days later."

"Okay, so?"

"Well, where do all the ladders start?"

He stopped walking. "Huh. I don't know. That's a good question. But I guess they must be around here somewhere, right? Unless you think the Refurserkir got rid of—"

"Just a second," I interrupted. "Be quiet... Did you hear something?"

He cocked his head to listen.

"Hear something like what?" he whispered back. "Not like a pipe bursting, right?"

"No, I—" I stopped mid-sentence to peer into the darkness behind us and listen a bit more closely.

"I don't hear anything," Nathan whispered after a few seconds.

"Precisely. It's too quiet. Like the sound that the Refurserkir don't make. We'd better keep moving." I started back down the tunnel. "So how long have you been down here?" I asked.

Nathan didn't answer. Nor did I hear his footsteps. I stopped, but I didn't turn around.

"Nathan?" I said.

"So, are you too pusillanimous, then, to face me to my face?" came the response.

"Freysgoð," I pronounced, still refusing to turn. "I can't believe this."

"With certainty, it is I, though I do comprehend your incapacity to believe. You are indubitably perplexed by the modishness of my elocution. And yet that is only the inception of the variances that you will discern in me. Oh yes. A plethora has changed since I departed from you."

"What do you want?" I asked.

"Rotate to face me."

"I really have no desire to look at you right now."

"Rotate to face me or I will percolate your companion."

"I think you mean 'perforate,'" I said, turning but keeping my eyes lowered. I just didn't want to see him. Not here, not part of all this.

"You constructed me to feel unintelligent in the past, however you are incapable of doing so any longer. I do not aspire for your approval. I am the deity of my nation, and I will elocute as I will."

I finally looked up at him, then. In the darkness, with only the vague orange glow of the streetlamp above to see him by, it seemed to me that he hardly looked anything at all like the man I'd married. But then I realized that I was wrong. The only difference was in the accessories; he was adorned now in fox fur and held a knife much like the one that Gerd had used to remove my finger. Otherwise, he was exactly the same: big and blond, with a perpetually manic gleam in his eyes that I'd always taken as a sign of his boyish sense of wonder. I guess I'd just never looked that closely before. Nathan was lying on the ground behind him.

"I hope you and Gerd are happy," I said. "You know, for a long while I wanted to believe that she'd somehow brainwashed you, or played on your gullibility. I mean, I gave you the benefit of the doubt when you almost married her the first time.[46] But this is who you are; I see that now."

"Do not endeavor to revise me. You may never have comprehended me in the past, however do not contemplate that

---

46. See *Experts Texperts*, Vol. 8 of the *Memoirs*.

you may abruptly comprehend me now, even considering the novel modishness of my elocution."

"What do you want?" I asked flatly. "Are you going to kill me?"

"I am not the bad one. I aspire for you to perceive the veracity of this. You and your family were always the bad ones, who reciprocated great ills to my nation."

"Do you mean 'precipitated great ills'?" I asked.

"Whether I have fully assimilated my newly modish vocabulary is not—" He stopped mid-sentence to look down at the ground. I looked, as well, to see what was so interesting. It was hard to make out in the darkness, but there was something moving around his feet.

"Can it be?" Prescott said, kneeling down. "It is you. Garm, my dog."

I stepped closer. It was really Garm. My neck shivered with adrenaline and I almost laughed. He was standing on two legs to try to lick Prescott's face.

"Here is the only veritably noble affiliate of your family," Prescott said, leaning farther down to allow Garm to lick him more fully. And then Garm bit his nose.

He put his hand to his face as he yelled in pain, and he knocked Garm away, toward me. "You have even turned my dog against me," he muttered. And then Nathan kicked him in the head before he could rise to his feet.

"Come on," Nathan said rushing past me as I knelt to pick up Garm.

"I missed you," I whispered to my dog. But this was no time for a teary reunion, even though Prescott seemed to be out cold. I followed Nathan as quickly as I could with a dog cradled in my arms. After less than a minute of running, however, the tunnel came abruptly to an end.

"Fuck," Nathan said. "Fuck, fuck, fuck." He slammed his fist against the wall each time he said the word; it made a hollow sound that only highlighted how silent it had become again.

I ran my right hand frantically over the wall in front of us, hoping for something...

The wall was blank. I couldn't even make out any pipes. In fact—as nearly as I could tell in what little light we had—it was unadorned completely, the only exception being a small piece of handle-shaped metal sticking out about waist-level near the wall's right edge.

It struck me slowly.

"It's a door!" I yelled. And the handle actually turned.

The room that opened up on the door's other side was darker than the tunnel had been, but we entered it anyway and I slammed the door behind us.

"Anybody home?" Nathan called into the blackness.

There was no answer, but the room sounded rather small.

Feeling our way slowly across, we found the far wall about eight feet away, and there was a second door—wooden—in its center.

That door, however, was locked. A dead end after all.

"Damnation!"

"Well, at least we made it this far," Nathan offered.

"Not good enough. Help me look for a key," I said.

I set Garm on the floor and felt around the doorframe, fruitlessly, and then we spread out. Against the right wall, I bumped into what must have been a big wooden desk.

Drawers. Papers, pens, and clips within. Something heavy and leathern thereon.

"Come here, help me push this. We can at least stop anyone else from getting in here, even if we don't manage to get out."

We managed to get it against the door we'd come through. The desk drawers were facing toward us, and so I started to rummage, still hoping to find a key. But then behind me I suddenly heard Nathan throw his body up against the other door.

"Ungh! Ow. That *was* my good shoulder... Damn. What are we going to do?"

I sat down on the desktop and resisted the urge to hold my head with bloody hands. I definitely could feel the hyper-clarity of the ormolu slipping away now.

"I don't know," I said. "I just really wish my father were here."

"Oh. About your father..." Nathan said, and then he got very quiet.

"What?" I asked. "Have you seen him?"

"Yeah, just a little before I found you, in fact."

"Is he okay?"

"He's— Well, I don't know. Just let me start at the beginning."

He told me, then, the story of how he had managed to end up down in the steam tunnels. He said that he first began to suspect that something was rotten, so to speak, in the state of New Uruk when he finally placed one of the names that Philip Leshio had mentioned earlier when he'd invited me to Hrothgar's. "'Mutt' Sanders." Nathan had thought it sounded familiar at the time, but it took a lot of bouncing it around in his head for him to recall that it was the name of a minor character from a movie that he'd played in back when he was a kid.

All of the sudden—like an epiphany—it dawned on him. The name was a clue from Surt, who must have seen him out walking with me that morning... And who must also have been the mastermind behind the dognapping. Hence 'Mutt'! Which also played into and contrasted with Iceland's whole thing about genetic purity and... Well, it worked on so many levels, it just had to be true, and so Nathan decided to head to Hrothgar's straight away just to make sure I was okay.

Unfortunately, he had managed to get himself a little lost on his way up to the graveyard for the candlelit vigil. So he went into a gas station to ask for directions. This turned out to be fairly fortuitous, though, because while he was in there he saw a newspaper with Shirley's face on the front, and he realized that she was actually this woman that he'd met in Denmark and Vanaheim, and it hadn't been a long leap from there to put the whole thing together with her character in the *Memoirs*... And so the fact that someone from the *Memoirs* had been murdered only reinforced his idea that Surt must indeed be involved in all of this somehow. Despite the fact that he had supposedly died.

So he got direction from the attendant, and he started walking. And that's when he saw Garm—or at least he was sure that it was a dachshund—chasing a fox down the street. He ran after them, of course, until he saw them both disappear down a broken sewer grate. This all struck him as rather odd, but he thought it might also be somehow significant, so he stopped to examine the sewer grating. But then he was abducted by the Refurserkir.

They just appeared out of nowhere. In fact, it was as if—

prior to appearing—they actually summoned up a sort of substantial nowhere precisely so that they could emerge from it. Like suddenly he felt as if there were a lack of space around him—not even a vacuum, but... Well, whatever it was, the Refurserkir popped out of it.

Before he knew what had happened, though, they'd covered his head in a fox-fur sack. So he couldn't see exactly where he was being taken, and in fact he didn't even really have a sense of the direction he was being dragged in. In retrospect, he assumed it must have been down the nearest manhole, but when they removed the sack so that he could see again, he just found himself in this huge subterranean auditorium. If he hadn't known better, he would have thought it was some modernized section of Vanaheim. It certainly didn't seem like the sort of thing that one would expect to find beneath New Crúiskeen. In fact, it looked like they'd only recently knocked out a few pillars and maybe a whole level of tunnels just to make space for it.

They just tied him to one of the pillars that remained and left him there for a while.

He had no idea at the time why he was important enough to be abducted, and no one would talk to him at all. All the Refurserkir made him think of Prescott, though, and so his initial idea had been that maybe Prescott had somehow gotten the idea that Nathan was trying to "move in" on me. Which couldn't be further from the truth, of course; he was a married man, for one thing, and— But the truth of the situation was all revealed later, after they had already dragged my father out to the altar to be sacrificed—

"Sacrificed?"

"Yeah... I'm getting ahead of myself, though."

"But he's okay?"

"Well... Just let me explain."

"..."

"So—"

"And you're married?"

"Oh. Well, yeah. I thought you knew that... I've got a daughter, too. She's beautiful. She just turned two and a half yesterday, actually... But, I'm sorry—back to what happened—you probably already get the point of where this whole story is headed, but..."

"Believe me, I don't."

"Well—like I was saying—it turned out that Prescott was gonna sacrifice your father in order to complete his ascension to godhood or something,[47] but your dad—who initially seemed completely spaced out—got this sudden burst of energy and started fighting back as they were trying to tie him down... I think he knocked Prescott unconscious. But that was enough of a diversion for me to break free—because I'd already sawed through my straps using the jagged corner of the pillar that I was tied to—and so then I immediately

---

47. As mentioned above, somewhere, the name "Freysgoð" is actually a title of some religious significance to the Vanatru. The rite of ascension referred to here is the ceremony during which the ascendant, vernal Freysgoð, at the age of puberty, takes the place in society of his father: the previous, autumnal Freysgoð. This traditionally entails the ritual sacrifice of the father, but—as related in Volume 3 of *The Memoirs of Emily Bean* (the title of which I shall not give, as it verbally plays upon Our Heroine's pseudonym, which is otherwise omitted from this text)—Prescott's own ascension was disrupted by the untimely arrival of Our Heroine, and his father died of natural causes before the ritual could be resumed.

made a dash to help him—your dad... He was fending off the attacks of about five Refurserkir by himself, already. With what looked like a steak knife."

"But you helped him?"

"I was going to. Surt got in my way, though. I didn't know who he was, at first, but then we had this big swordfight, with the ceremonial blades that Prescott had been planning to use in the sacrifice of your father... The training that I did for the final scene of *Hamlet* really came in handy, there, though I did get a pretty nasty cut on my shoulder... But while we were fighting, I realized who he was, because he started telling me all about his plan. He talked quite a bit while he fought. He can be a bit wordy."

"Oh yeah?"

"Yeah, but so he was just going off about Shirley MacGuffin, and how I guess she'd 'belittled' him or something. I don't know exactly what she did, but he was somehow under the impression that she had told me something about him while I was in Vanaheim, and he said that she shouldn't have embarrassed him that way... Which I guess is why he had the Refurserkir abduct me. I didn't really know what he was talking about, though, and he probably embarrassed himself more in his babbling than anything, because Shirley never actually got the chance to tell me much of anything at all."

Nathan coughed emphatically before continuing.

"He talked about you a little, too... I'm not sure exactly what he meant, but he said that he was just doing all of this to *help* you, and that—"

"I don't want to hear it," I said. "Just tell me about my father. Is he okay?"

"Well, you see, right in the middle of everything—while I was fighting Surt—a snowplow fell through the ceiling, and it brought a bunch of snow and street down with it... And that pretty much cut me off from everybody else around. Luckily there was a tunnel nearby for me to escape into, and I—"

"But what happened to my father?"

"I'm sorry," he said. "I really am..." His voice was suddenly solemn.

"Sorry about what? What are you saying?"

"I mean—" he began.

But before he could elaborate there was a knock upon the door opposite the one we'd come through.

"We're in here!" Nathan shouted out.

And a moment after that the door was shattered into splinters of wood and light... It stung my eyes into a sudden squint, and when I could open them wide again the first things I noticed were the dust particles floating in the air all around us.

And then I saw what lay beyond the door, and I realized where we were.

"It is very good that you are here," Blaise said, poking his head through the huge hole he'd made in the door. "But you should come out now and join the rest of us in the parlor."

CHAPTER FOUR

"What is this place?" Nathan asked as we stepped through the shattered doorway.

"Hubert Jorgen's house," I told him, leaning down to pick up Garm. And then, as it dawned on me more completely: "The Bluebeard basement door! That room must have been his workshop... And I don't suppose it's a coincidence that it connects up with the tunnels where the Refurserkir have made their lair, either... I guess that sort of seals it for Hubert, then. Or it would if he weren't dead."

"Bluebeard what?" Nathan asked. "Seals how? Who's Hubert, again? And what sort of workshop?"

I chose not to answer. Blaise beckoned us to follow him up the stairs and on to the parlor.

I'd always considered the parlor to be one of the stranger rooms in Hubert's house. It was anachronistic—difficult to reconcile with the rest of his taste. Lots of red plush and mahogany. Two epees hanging over a plaster bust of Orson Welles upon the mantelpiece. There was a glass case in the corner displaying a collection of Meerschaum pipes, each of which was imbrued by a different blend of tobacco (labeled). Yet Hubert neither fenced nor smoked.

Blaise entered ahead of us and hung his door-smashing hammer[48] on the far wall along with the rest of the Vanaheimic weaponry of Hubert's collection. As Nathan and I followed him in I saw that quite a coterie was assembled there already. Wible and Pacheco were slumped on a loveseat to the doorway's left, Constance Lingus sat in a large plush armchair, and my father was there, beside her, on a small sofa by the drinks table.

His white hair was ruffled, but otherwise he appeared unharmed. I didn't move. I felt woozy.

"Dad..." I said. "You're all right."

"Yes, yes, dear thing," he said dismissively. "I am fine. It is nice to see that you are fine, as well."

"I found him wandering around downtown near where that snowplow fell through the street," Connie said.

"You made me think he was dead!" I yelled at Nathan.

"No, I just— I didn't know. That's all I meant. I was completely cut off from everyone else down there. So I didn't get to see what happened to him. And before that I was kind of engrossed in my swordfight, so... I'm sorry." He sounded almost meek.

I turned to the rest of the room. "What's going on here?

48. Actually a Viking battle-axe, a gift that Jorgen received from the Master himself.

Why are all of you in Hubert's house?"

"My partner and I have been here since shortly after our meeting with you this afternoon. As we informed you at that time, we believe the librarian to possess some knowledge regarding—"

"I discovered them tethered by ropes to bedposts in an upstairs room," Blaise clarified, taking a seat beside my father.

I noticed then that Garm was licking my hands, so I set him down on the floor. He ran over to curl up at my father's feet. "And the rest of you?" I asked.

"Your hands," Blaise replied. "The blood. Are you all right?"

"We'll talk about my hands later." I found my gloves still stuffed into my jacket pocket and pulled them quickly on. "But perhaps we should start a fire, first."

"It is certainly cold in this room," Pacheco said, "however—"

"Well, if someone has some matches we can remedy that," I interrupted. I rubbed a sleeve across my bloodshot eyes. I could feel the swollen veins within them.

Nathan followed me over to the fireplace, and he poked through the ashes before throwing on a couple of logs and some kindling from the pile beside. Wible came over, too, and offered up his box of matches; within a few minutes we had the beginnings of a good fire going.

"So how much do you all know? What brought you here?" I asked.

"I came to find Hubert Jorgen," Blaise answered. "I believe—"

"Wait a second; hold on." I was confused, and I shook my head rapidly to communicate the point. "I thought Hubert was dead. Is it not true that Hubert is dead? Did you not find his body?"

"I did, in the Two-Story House, but it disappeared again before I could verify its lack of life. He had no pulse, and yet... That is why I came here, perhaps to find him."

I put my left hand to my forehead to steady myself but then quickly removed it, fearful that blood would seep through the glove. "Let me get this perfectly straight," I said. "You're telling me that Hubert might be alive after all?"

"I do not know. I felt certain that his body was lifeless, and yet... I do not know. But I believe that his possible murderer and the murderer of my wife may both be the same man, and this is also why I have come here. You mentioned Jorgen to me earlier in connection with her. Furthermore, the Two-Story House describes a murder, and... I believe that Shirley, when she was in Denmark a few years ago— I believe that Hubert Jorgen may have been the one who—"

"Oh," I said, his meaning becoming abruptly clear, albeit only to me and my drug-addled mind. "Oh... No, Blaise. He wasn't."

"You do not know what I mean; I am not making myself clear."

"No, you're not, but I think I do know what you mean. And you're wrong."

"I think I'm a little lost here," Nathan said, grabbing the poker and stoking the fire. It was already blazing quite nicely, although I still felt rather cold. "Who's this Hubert guy? I thought this whole thing was about whoever murdered that Shirley girl, and Prescott trying to kill your father, and burning down his library, and stealing your dog."

"Do you know the name of he who killed my wife?" Blaise asked Nathan, raising his voice almost to a shout. "If so, we must find him immediately."

"Actually Blaise, I think *I* know his name," I said.

He almost leapt out of his seat at this. "Why did you not tell me this before?"

"Well, when I saw you earlier I still didn't know," I said. I looked down then, avoiding his gaze, and began toying with my empty glove finger. "Though I suppose I should admit that I did have a vague idea about *why* Shirley might have been killed. And I didn't tell you. It was the last thing Shirley asked of me, though—specifically not to tell you—and since I wasn't sure at the time that it definitely had anything to do with her death... I mean, it was just a vague idea..."

Blaise was just staring at me white-faced when I looked back up. "But now—" he began.

"Just wait a second," I interrupted. "I want to clarify something up front. You seem to be under the impression that Shirley was cheating on you. I want to assure you that she wasn't."

"But just what was this vague idea you had, then?" Connie blurted before Blaise could say anything.

"Well," I said, keeping an eye on him as I spoke. "I'd known for a long time that something horrible happened while Shirley was in Denmark a few years ago. Something involving... another person. But Shirley only ever hinted at it. She never told me exactly what it was until a few nights ago. And even then she still didn't reveal the identity of the other person involved. But she did tell me that she was planning on confronting this other person. And I thought that that sounded like a good idea, based on what she had told me—like it would help her get over the whole thing. So I didn't stop her... And that was the last time I saw her."

"Well, that certainly is vague."

"I'm sorry, but she made me promise that I wouldn't tell anyone," I said, rubbing my temples and trying to ignore Connie. "And I think I have to respect her last wish. And you know, earlier, like I said, I didn't know for a fact that what happened in Denmark had anything to do with her murder—she might not have confronted the person yet, for all I knew. And—even if she had—that didn't necessarily mean that the person she confronted was the murderer. And so I figured that if the police could solve the case without any of this coming out... I mean, how could I tell the police if I couldn't tell Blaise? I just couldn't betray Shirley's final trust."

"I appreciate your loyalty," Blaise said, settling back into his seat, his face unnaturally pale and devoid of expression. "But of necessity that loyalty must now be superseded."

"What does all of this have to do with Prescott and Vanaheim and all of that?" Nathan asked, grabbing my arm to hold me up as I leaned perhaps too far to one side.

"Ah," I said, raising the gloved index finger of my right hand. I put my left hand behind my back; it felt almost as if it had been dipped in syrup. "That's where things get interesting. You see, Wible and Pacheco, here, were actually hired by Shirley herself."

"How—" Wible began.

"Because Shirley herself told me that she planned to hire you guys. She thought somebody was trying to stop her from writing the Thomas Kyd version of *Hamlet*, because someone had broken into her house and stolen a bunch of her research.

But actually it was her draft of the Vanaheimic *Hamlet* that they had been after. And that's safe and sound in my house. You see, Gerd—"

"Enough of this," Blaise bellowed, to which Garm offered a bark of critique. "You must just tell me how this is related to the death of my wife."

"I—" I suddenly lost my breath, then, and I felt as if I could cry. All over again. I realized that I'd been so busy trying to explain everything that I'd almost forgotten Shirley was really dead.

"Well, the murderer was working with Gerd," I said, clenching my eyes and trying to remain calm. "I was just getting to that. But the *Hamlet* thing—admittedly, that's not why he did it. It was just a sick old man and his wounded pride... He was the one who—" But then I looked at Connie.

"No, I'm sorry, but I'm just going to have to explain all of this to you later, Blaise," I said. "In private. Because you're the only one who needs to know about this part. Some things need to remain personal."[49] I squinted my eyes at Connie then and waved an admonishing finger at her.

"Okay. You're obviously drunk," Connie said, slapping the cushy arm of her chair. "I mean, what is the point of all of this? If you actually do know who killed Shirley, could you please just slur it to us already? Or, better yet, slur it to the

---

49. This is the third of the aforementioned semi-significant absences. Though Our Heroine claims, here, that she knows what this secret is and that she will "explain [it] later," I can find no place in the text where she exhibits the slightest knowledge of said secret. One must conclude that she is a liar. Does she know what happened in Denmark? Doubtful. I would contend, rather, that her assertion to the contrary is included for the sole purpose of tormenting me with the possibility that she knows something that I do not.

police... No, scratch that; tell me and *then* tell the police. But spit it out!"

I stuck my tongue between my teeth and gave her my most lethal glare.

"It was Surt who did these things!" my father suddenly yelled.

"Well," I said, trying again to straighten up, "you're all aware of my father's feelings on the subject."

No one responded, though I felt all of their eyes upon me. Fourteen, counting Garm.

"All right. Fine," I said. "It *was* Surt. He helped Gerd with her plan, he was in Denmark with Shirley, and he killed Shirley when she confronted him about what he'd done to her there. It was Surt all along." I stumbled a bit then, in a momentary swoon, and in my grab at the mantel for support, I accidentally knocked off Hubert's plaster bust of Orson Welles. It shattered and scattered across the floor. I'm afraid this may have looked like a dramatic gesture.

"Well, what a shocker," Connie replied in what she must have imagined was a dry tone.

I shook my head, then, perhaps a tad too rapidly.

"No... You don't understand. That's not the end. I know who Surt really is," I tried to tell her.

At least that's what went through my head.

But that was the point at which I fell to the floor.

A wave of pleasure whelmed over me.

"God, I'm calling an ambulance," I heard Connie say.

My whole body felt dead—like an arm that had been slept on—but my mind was active, looking out of it, at all of these legs and feet moving toward me, at Garm licking me, at broken pieces of Orson Welles strewn all around me... But I didn't care about any of it; I was euphoric.

Wible and Pacheco grabbed me by the armpits and helped me to my feet, and—after a brief vision of the color red—sensation prickled back into my limbs.

"I'm sorry," I said. "I've been drugged and stuff."

"It is okay," someone answered. "You should sit down."

So they set me down, then, in the big plush chair that Connie had been sitting in.

"An ambulance is on its way," she announced, coming into the room through the hall door. I didn't realize she'd been gone.

"No. I do not want this," I said. "I'm fine. I just need some fresh air."

Nathan peeled the wet glove from my left hand, and I looked. Just plopped there bloody on the armrest, the hand didn't resemble anything. Though I half-expected it to start flopping around.

"I need to go outside," I said.

"I think you should probably just sit here until the ambulance arrives," Nathan told me.

"No." I was trying to speak clearly. "I will go to the hospital. I will get into an ambulance and go there. But I really don't want to wait in here before I do so."

"Regardless of what you want," Connie said, "I think that waiting in here would be the wisest thing for you to do."

"No," I told her. "You think wrong. It would be wiser for me to wait outside. I should cool my body down. Make my blood flow less freely."

None of them were medically expert enough to argue with

the logic of this, so after only a moment's hesitation Wible and Pacheco helped me stand again, and I walked of my own power out to the porch.

Everyone followed me out, then. Even my dad, who was strangely silent. And the night was beautiful—black and blue and cold. But I was still feeling a bit giddy.

I was feeling ecstatic, actually—out of myself, and I wanted to finish telling them everything, finish bringing it all out into the open; I had to turn around and grab hold of *somebody*. Which I did—tightly by the shoulders—and then I whispered to him the final secret.[50] That it was Magnus. That the author of all my mother's mysteries had been the villain behind many of them. That *he'd* been the one who murdered Shirley. That he was the true face behind the many masks of Surt and that he always had been.[51]

And as I explained it, I suddenly realized that it didn't

---

50. Who? Whom? To whom did she whisper this? And what did he do with this information (surely a lie though it was)? Furthermore, was this mindless slander on her part, or was it carefully calculated toward a more terrible effect? After all, though Our Heroine claims throughout the novel to be entirely unmotivated by such petty concerns as desire for revenge, surely she was aware that others in the company were not so civilized; Valison was strangled shortly after the events of this novel, and it is my belief that Our Heroine indirectly killed him with this whisper, planting the idea in the mind of the true murderer. She will not deceive me as she did once before.

51. The suggestion, here—that Magnus Valison was the true identity of the arch-criminal, Surt—must, finally, exterminate any possible belief in the validity of this text. Anyone who ever met the man in the final years of his life can attest to the fact that he had neither the disposition nor the physical ability to perform any of the deeds ascribed to Surt in the *Memoirs*, and this suggestion to the contrary betrays the novel's heavy reliance on the reportage of "Constance Lingus," who—not long after the period of the novel's action—suggested a similar thesis in her weekly tabloid column. She elaborated this

matter to me that he had gotten away. He'd said he'd done all of this for me; to give me "meaning." By playing the detective to his villain, I supposed. But I would not be defined in relation to him. I wanted to whisper that last part to somebody, too. But then I immediately felt as if I were going to be sick, and I stumbled off of the porch, into the snowy yard.

And I was dizzy.

"I do not want this," I said, hunched over and holding my head in my bloody hands.

"You don't want what?" Connie asked, coming quickly up beside me and wrapping her arm around my back.

I stood upright and took a deep breath, considering all the possible answers to that question. "I don't know," I mumbled.

But it struck me as somehow profound. This series of

---

claim into its most libelous form during the course of the already-cited article in which she published excerpts of Shirley MacGuffin's supposed Vanaheimic version of the Hamlet story. The Reader will forgive me if I question Miss Lingus's journalistic integrity and if I suggest that—in constructing this "factually based" fiction—the Author should have stuck more closely to the confirmable facts. Bear in mind that I, of all people, should know if there were any truth in this assertion. Being so close to Magnus Valison and so knowledgeable on the subject of Surt, I think I would have known if they were the same person. Never mind how, but I would have known.

Valison, doubtless, felt an affinity with his anonymous villain to the extent that any writer identifies with his most strongly rendered characters—it would be pointless to deny this—but to infer the two men's mutual identity from this affinity and then to present it as fact is insulting not only to the memory of Valison but to the intelligence of the Reader. One may as well assert that Milton was the Devil or that Conan Doyle was Moriarty. So it is my sincere hope that the intelligent Reader will therefore take this assertion as nothing more than the misguided fiction that it is. He would have told me. One of him. It simply cannot be true. It cannot. It can't.

negations. Things that I did not want... To go back to teaching next semester and deal with people like Boris Baxter.[52] To be the heroine of mystery novels as my mother was. To experience the intensity of life only through contrast... I did not want Prescott, Hubert, or Nathan.[53] On a more immediate level, I did not particularly want to go to the hospital; I didn't want to go the night without Garm by my side.

Standing there with Connie, waiting for the ambulance that would not restore my finger, I felt the air vivid and crisp around me. The sky was clear and starry with a bright full moon; the snow was all fallen, and it was dry beneath my feet.

The low angle of the porch light behind me threw my shadow out across it, reproducing my shape in such epic length and detail that I could almost make out my individual features. As I squinted at it, there was nothing missing at all. I broke away from Connie then and jogged out into it—I stooped to stick my bare hand into it—and the cold of it stole my breath and clarified my thoughts with adrenaline. The snow and shadow.

And even when the ambulance rounded the corner, and I straightened back up and raised my frozen hand to signal them—"It's me; here I am"—my shadow was there, too, waving back at me like someone I knew.

My shadow was waving at me furiously, as if it were someone whom I hadn't seen in a very long time.

---

52. At least one of her wishes came true.

53. I should have guessed that she was a lesbian.

AFTERWORD

Concerning the Origin and Authorship of Icelander

Magnus Valison left behind a forest's-worth of papers, and in his will he appointed me—John Treeburg—with the bewildering task of sorting through it all. And yet it wasn't until late 2004—over three years after his death—that these papers were finally planted upon my desk. This unfortunate delay was mostly due to a mix-up involving a spurious copy of the Master's will that listed Jon Ymirson as literary executor rather than myself. Yet once I proved in court that this document was a forgery, despite "Our Heroine's" feeble attempts to discredit me, I immediately retrieved the precious papers from Ymirson's guilty hands and began to dig my way through them.

At first I was taken aback by the mountains of papers that piled up on my floor, though, and it was some time before I developed an appropriate system of organization for them, much less discovered any of the literary gems buried within. As happenstance would have it, of course, the typescript of the novel in question was located in the nethermost stratum of one of those mountains, and consequently it wasn't until nearly a month later—in January of 2005—that I unearthed it. The pile under which it was buried was a particularly large one that consisted mostly of jotted phone numbers, lists of Things To Do, enigmatic phrases scrawled on the backs of grocery receipts (what did Valison want with dog food when he had no dog?), and unfinished missives to friends. As soon as I recognized that this was a novelization of recent events, though, I could scarcely contain the hopes that rose up within me.

"Could this be Valison's rumored final work?" I wondered.

The answer that I have since arrived at is an unequivocal "no." Despite certain superficial similarities of style and content, I am convinced that this text can be nothing more than the work of a talented pretender—a lode of iron pyrite found among veins of gold—and the typescript must have been introduced into the collection of Valison's papers at some point after they were initially entrusted to Jon Ymirson. Ymirson himself proved no help with regard to this matter, as he refused so much as to speak with me. But I am sure that his condition has rendered him a moron by now, regardless. Without anything more in the way of hard evidence, though, the typescript's origin must nominally remain obscure.

Now, there are undoubtedly those who would still contend that this novel is indeed the work of Magnus Valison, seemingly without any more basis than the fact that it would appear to be the simplest supposition. Yet such theories fail to account for the multiple references to belts within the text itself, which clearly indicate an intimate familiarity with the circumstances of Valison's death and perhaps even point toward the identity of his murderer. I am, of course, the first to admit the infinitely supreme nature of the Master's talent, but even I do not suppose that he could have written a novel containing the details of his own death.

Without question, the Author's main purpose seems to be to twist events—to confuse me—and I believe that a close reading of the text will bear me out on this assertion. Why else would this Author have ended the text in this place, when all of the best bits were yet to come?

Surt's anger, for instance, when he discovered that the *Hamlet* (or, more precisely, *Amleth*, as Saxo Grammaticus would have it, and as any good forger would have known) manuscript that had been stolen from Shirley MacGuffin's house had been nothing more than a straight translation of Saxo; Prescott and Gerd's suddenly enforced flight when Jon Ymirson threw off his idiocy long enough to persuade the Refurserkir to turn on their masters; or before all of that, even, when Hubert Jorgen miraculously appeared at Our Heroine's side in the back of the ambulance, assuring the EMTs that she had expressly requested his presence there. She hadn't contradicted him, and in fact she'd even grabbed his hand as he proceeded to reveal the true twist of the story—that he had merely used an old Refurserkir trick to slow his heartbeat, in order to fake his death and thus escape the possible wrath of Surt (it was a fate he had mistakenly come to fear since hearing of Shirley MacGuffin's death—because who knew what other loose ends the Master might want to tie up?). He had meant to lead her to the Two-Story House, where she would have discovered his body.

Our Heroine, of course, made the ridiculous suggestion that she had suspected this turn of events since the moment that Duplain had mentioned the fact that Jorgen's body had gone missing—she knew about Jorgen's fascination with the Refurserkir, she explained, and that he had spent considerable time with them while in Vanaheim. Yet if she truly was aware of this much, she nonetheless could not have been aware of everything.

Indeed, she continued to affect a false compassion for Jorgen even as he inwardly reveled in the glory of what he still thought had been accomplished. This was, of course, before anyone realized how implausible the text of the *Amleth* manuscript was or that—far from "getting away with it"—Gerd and Prescott would eventually return to their homeland in disgrace while Surt—the Master himself—would to all appearances die (yet again) within the next few days.

"But how did you get involved in this?" she had asked Jorgen at the time. She was delirious, perhaps, but it came across a delirious sort of kindness, which Jorgen found horribly sickening. "Were you Surt's understudy or something? I mean, I know that you were always fascinated with his skill, and you probably just wanted to learn from him, but..." She slipped into unconsciousness before she could complete this condescending sentence.

The mere suggestion, though! After all, had Jorgen been deeply involved in the supposed Vanaheimic forgery scheme—which has never been convincingly established—it would have been in the role of master, not understudy. His work at that point would have surpassed anything that Surt could even have dreamt of doing. Particularly since the man was approaching his centennial birthday, and palsy tolls the forger's hand...

But Jorgen did not let such underestimation disturb him. He knew how useful it could be. In fact, her comment set him off on a fit of introspection. He had sneaked into the ambulance solely with the intention of bidding Our Heroine farewell, yet her words had served to remind him both of his capabilities and his calling. No, he would not slink away to start a new life simply for the safety of it! He would embrace his fate! He left Our Heroine at the hospital entrance and proceeded on foot back toward his home, hoping as he walked that the party of unwelcome houseguests would have had the time and inclination to disband by the time he got there. Of course, he was in for a bit of a surprise on that score.

Apparently the Refurserkir had arrived at his home just moments before he did, pouring in huge numbers through the door in his basement. Watching the scene unfold through his drawing room window, then, Jorgen saw Blaise Duplain wildly swinging the

Viking battle axe that had hung above the mantel, maintaining a perimeter within which Constance Lingus, Wible, and Pacheco cowered for safety. He saw the oafish Prescott trying to command the Refurserkir from the safety of the drawing room doorway as Our Heroine's precious wonder-whelp nipped at his feet. And most amazing of all was Jon Ymirson, clambering atop one of Jorgen's tables, spreading his arms and swelling with fury before letting loose a mighty shout that reverberated in Jorgen's eardrums, outside of the house though he was. The Refurserkir had all ceased fighting, then, and looked to Ymirson. And then he began to speak. Jorgen couldn't hear the exact words he said, of course, but... Well, I am going on too long.

So, against my better judgment, I have allowed this version of things to stand, exactly as its Author composed it. I have, regardless, exposed the truth beneath all of the falsehoods, not to mention the vice-versa. I no longer have any fear. No one cannot hurt me now with the doubts that they would sow. They think they have won. But oh, no.

ACKNOWLEDGMENTS

For late-night conversations and general inspiration: Rizvan Khawar, Jason Ko, Trevor Perrin, Tony Sertich, and Scott Zorsch.

For lending their eyes when no one else was looking: Steve Margulis, Tony Palermo, Michael Peterson, Chris Coleman, Alex Paknadel, William Vollmann and Jason Woliner.

For life, etcetera: Jim and Beverly Long, Bill and Betty Parsons, Mel and Jean Ireland, Don and Juanita Long.

For Twist-a-plots and comic books: Jaysen Long.

For putting up with me and sometimes even playing along: Devon Kurcina.

For invaluable support, and for Chantal: The Clarkes—Keith, Margot, Liz, Anne, and Caro.

For making the world a better place: The Longs—Katie, Samantha, and Haley. The Kurcina—Dave. And Mackerel.

For lessons learned: Ron Loewinsohn, Clark Blaise, Bharati Mukherjee, Chris Nealon, Alyce Miller, Terri Parent, and Samrat Upadhyay.

For keen insight into nearly everything: Eli Horowitz.

For additional insight: Jordan Bass, Greg Larson, Jim Fingal, Mac Barnett, Caroline Loevner, Gabe Hudson, and Kevin Feeney.

For constant companionship and support; for providing the foundation on which this novel was built; for humor, love, and perpetual wit: my wife, Chantal Clarke.